OBEDIENCE

Other Dave Brandstetter Novels

Early Graves
The Little Dog Laughed
Nightwork
Gravedigger
Skinflick
The Man Everybody Was Afraid Of
Troublemaker
Death Claims
Fadeout

Also by Joseph Hansen

Bohannon's Book (stories)
Steps Going Down
Brandstetter & Others (stories)
Pretty Boy Dead
Job's Year
Backtrack
A Smile in His Lifetime
The Dog & Other Stories
One Foot in the Boat (verse)

OBEDIENCE

A DAVE BRANDSTETTER MYSTERY

JOSEPH HANSEN

THE MYSTERIOUS PRESS

New York • London • Tokyo

This is a work of fiction. Any similarity between the characters depicted herein and actual living people is pure coincidence.

The Mysterious Press, 129 West 56th Street, New York, N.Y. 10019

Printed in the United States of America

First Printing: November 1988

10 9 8 7 6 5 4 3 2 1

Library of Congress Cataloging-in-Publication Data

Hansen, Joseph, 1923–
    Obedience : a David Brandstetter mystery.

    I. Title.
PS3558.A513O24   1988   813'.54   88-40072
ISBN 0-89296-296-8

For my brother Bob

1

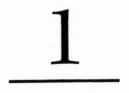e was quitting. But notifying all the insurance companies in the West he'd done death claims investigations for in recent years turned out to be a long job. He had sat down to do it after lunch, and was still typing away in a lonely little island of lamplight in the looming, raftered room when Cecil Harris walked in at midnight. A field reporter for television news, the tall, lanky young black lived with Dave. He ambled down the room, glanced over Dave's shoulder as he passed the desk, hung his jacket on the hat tree, and rattled glasses and bottles at the bar.

"I didn't mean for you to work so hard," he said. "Let me put that on our computer. You only need to write one letter. Give me the list of addresses. Send the same letter everyplace, just a different salutation each time."

Dave ground a finished sheet wearily out of the little typewriter, laid the page aside with its envelope, closed the case of the portable, put it into a deep lower drawer of the desk, and closed the drawer. He ached between the shoulder blades. "They'd know it was a form letter."

"There's a daisy-wheel printer in the program director's office. I can use it at night." Cecil handed Dave a Glenlivet on ice in a stocky glass. "Daisy-wheel printer—nobody would know it wasn't typed."

"I'd know," Dave said. "And no one deserves to be treated that way." He took off the glasses he used for reading and writing, and laid them on the desk. "Not even insurance executives." He stood, stretched, picked up his cigarettes and lighter from the desk, and carried these, with his drink, to the corduroy couch that faced the fireplace. He dropped onto it. Cecil sat down beside him and Dave put a light kiss on his mouth. "Thanks for the offer."

"Hell," Cecil said, "I was the one who talked you into it." For months, he had been asking Dave to quit. Dave's balking had been partly play-acting, but Cecil hadn't seen that, and now he was feeling guilty. He gave Dave a worried glance. "Up to me to try to make it easy, if I can."

"Don't sweat it," Dave said. "I'll work it out." He tasted the scotch, and lit a cigarette. "Why not look at it this way? I was sharpening my typing skills. To write my memoirs, right?" Cecil moaned. Dave changed the subject. "And what did you do today?"

Cecil took a breath. "Down in San Pedro County, there's a place I bet you never heard of. The Old Fleet marina." It had been there twenty-five years. Dave had heard of it, had even been there sometime, though he forgot why. But he didn't say this. Cecil sipped brandy, hummed gratefully at the taste, leaned his head back. "Half-dead factories and warehouses all around, windows smashed out. Oil derricks. Wobbly docks, posts all crusty with barnacles below the water. Water dark and greasy. Crowd of old boats, rusting away, rotting away. Some don't even have motors."

"A floating junkyard?" Dave said.

Cecil shook his head. "Home. People living on those boats." He sat forward, elbows on knees, turning the brandy snifter in long fingers, watching it glumly. "Been living there for years, some of them."

"And you drove down there with a camera crew?"

Cecil nodded. "Four this afternoon."

"What was the lead?" Dave said.

"The boat folks are being ousted. In sixty days. And most of them don't have the money to lease mooring spaces at good marinas."

"The good ones have waiting lists years long anyway," Dave said. "And they don't allow living on board."

"Right. The Old Fleet was the only one that did, and the only cheap one. But, even if there was another, those with no engines—they'd have to be towed there, and towing comes expensive." He shook his head, gloomily drank from the snifter. "Money sure can make people heartless."

"It's a five-thousand-year-old trend," Dave said. "Who has the money this time?"

"Name of Le Van Minh," Cecil said. "A Vietnamese importer. Lives here. Residency permit. He's owned the place for years. Now developers want to buy it, gentrify it, build condos all around, fancy restaurants and shops. The Old Fleet boaties are protesting. The protest was the news story, really. But they're poor. They can't win."

Dave said, "They probably couldn't win if they were rich." He snuffed his cigarette, knocked back the rest of his scotch, set down the glass. "These days, you see something you want—factory, fast-food outlet, super-market chain—and you've got the money, you get it, regardless of how the owner feels. It's called a hostile takeover." He pushed up off the couch. "Don't ask me to explain it."

"I don't guess Le minds selling," Cecil said. "He just owns it. I don't think it means anything to him. Just another investment. Don't suppose he ever saw it. Boat folks claim he only just heard there were people living there."

Dave winced and rubbed the back of his neck. "Dave, the demon typist, is tired," he said.

"Let's go to bed," Cecil said.

Dave walked in from the brick courtyard, the taste of coffee and blueberry muffins lingering in his mouth. He had just seen Cecil off to work in his flame-painted, blue-carpeted van. It was September, staffers were taking late vacations, Cecil was working double shifts this week. Dave ought to have factored that into his retirement plans. He had counted on Cecil's company during the days. Living alone he had never liked. He lit a cigarette, and leaned in the doorway, studying the room. Books had stacked up on the floor, against the pine plank walls. Books cluttered the brick surround of the fireplace, the desk and bar at the far end of the long room, the golden oak mission-style library table that stood behind the couch.

He had lived for years in this strange place on Horseshoe Canyon Trail—the two main buildings had started as stables, and in damp weather still smelled faintly of horse. But though Amanda, his very young stepmother, had put up open sleeping lofts here, had modernized the cook shack, installed clerestory windows and split-leveled the floor of the front building, Dave himself hadn't marked the place much. He'd been too busy. He had bought Navajo rugs for this building, some Mexican pottery pieces for the front building, but he'd never hung any pictures, and he liked pictures. He liked tall bookcases too, but the only ones here he'd slapped up back by the desk when he first moved in.

Well, now he wasn't busy anymore, was he? He had time to build all the bookshelves he wanted. This morning, while Cecil showered, Dave had signed, sealed, and stamped the letters, bundled them with a rubber band, and walked them out to the roadside box for the mailman to take away in his red, white, and blue jeep. Dave had made it official. The rest of his life was his own. And the first days of it, he was going to give to bookshelves and pictures—those watercolors by Larry Johns he'd bought last year, nice, loose, sure-handed sketches of the surf, rocks, dunes around the handsome beach house Johns shared with Tom Owens. Owens was an architect whose life Dave had saved a couple of times—the last time, because he'd put it in jeopardy.

He smiled grimly to himself, walked down the room and stood, head tilted, sizing up the long, knotty pine walls that flanked the fireplace. He liked the notion of bookshelves over, under, and around the windows. He turned, decided the pictures would look happiest lined up along the wall under the north sleeping loft. There was better height for the shelves on the fireplace wall. How many shelves? He had bought the lumber when he bought the place. It lay under blue plastic sheets sheltered by a vine-grown arbor at the back of the property. If termites and dry rot hadn't eaten it, there were probably enough board feet there. Dave needed a yardstick. Full of cheerful purpose, he started for the cook shack, where the tools were kept. And stopped.

A young woman stood in the doorway. He blinked at her. She carried a case, but he didn't think there was anything for sale in it. She was freckle-faced and sandy-haired, and wore a shirtmaker dress of crisp oyster-white twill with a floppy green bow at the throat. Her green-rimmed glasses were owlish, and she was doing her best to look prim and businesslike. He took her for a lawyer.

"Mr. Brandstetter," she said, "I'm Tracy Davis. Maybe you remember me. I used to work for Mr. Greenglass." She held out a business card. He went to her and took it, patted his shirt pocket, and remembered he'd left his reading glasses with the morning paper in the cook shack. Maybe the way he squinted at the card told her he couldn't read it. "Public Defender," she said, "San Pedro County. I need your help."

"Sorry." He held up both hands, took a backward step. "You're too late. As of this morning, I've retired."

The light went out of her face. "Oh, no."

"Don't feel bad," he said. "There are plenty of good investigators around." He started for his desk. "Come in. I'll write down some names and numbers for you."

She followed him. "It's not that. The Public Defender's office has its own investigators."

He sat at the desk, opened a drawer, brought out his address book. "Then what are you doing here?"

"I need the best," she said.

"That's very flattering but"—he shook his head—"what kind of retiree would I be if I only lasted one day at it? Would you respect a man like that?"

"I asked Mr. Greenglass to recommend someone, and he said you were the only choice. I've read about you in *Time, Newsweek, People.* Seen you on Ted Koppel, Oprah Winfrey, Phil Donahue. You're the best." She frowned. "Is it your health? You don't look sick."

"I'm fine." Dave switched on the desk lamp, found a pen, and, squinting to make out street and phone numbers, wrote them on the back of the card she'd given him. "But I won't be fine if I go back to work. I've been stabbed and shot, beaten up, burned out, half drowned, and run off roads too often lately. I'm tired of hospitals." He handed her the card. "My reflexes are slowing down, and everything ugly is speeding up. It's time I quit."

"But Mr. Greenglass promised me," she wailed. "If you don't save Andy Flanagan, no one will. No one else can."

"What makes Andy Flanagan so hard to save?"

"The man they say he killed is Vietnamese," she said, "and Andy lost his arm in Nam. And everyone who knows him knows he hates those people. To this very day. Thirteen years later. He is not a winning man. He's surly, full of hate and self-pity. He's a bigot and a bully."

"We don't put people in jail for those things." Dave stood up. "What's the evidence?"

She laughed hopelessly. "Oh, God. Where do I begin?"

"How about over a cup of coffee?" Dave said. "Cook shack is across the courtyard, there." He walked toward the sunlit front doorway. She followed. "What lovely rugs," she said. "Does this mean you'll take the case?"

"It means I'll listen to you," he said, "because I don't think anybody is going to shoot me for that. At least not right away."

Her heels rattled across old bricks scattered with the curled, dry leaves of the oak that spread its branches over the courtyard. "Listen and advise?" she wondered.

"Possibly." He pulled open the cook shack screen door and held it so she could duck inside under his arm. "But not consent," he said. Morning sunlight through tall windows dappled with leaf shadows the yellow enamel of cupboards. "Sit down." He waved a hand at a scrubbed deal table surrounded by plain pine chairs, and began putting together coffeemaker and coffee at a stately old nickel-plated range that cunningly hid the latest gadgetry. "You drove a long way to get here. You hungry?"

"Just coffee, please. No food." She pulled out a chair, sat down, slipped her shoulder bag off, and set it with the attaché case on the floor. "I'm too upset."

Dave took mugs down from a cupboard, spoons from a drawer. "New at this, are you?" He brought mugs, spoons, napkins to the table. "This your first homicide?"

She gave a bleak laugh. "I wish it were. But Andy Flanagan's my half-brother. He was a gentle, timid kid. Back then. The war changed him. None of the family wants anything to do with him now." Her eyes behind the big lenses pleaded up at him. "It's why I came to you. Andy is all mouth. He wouldn't kill anybody. At bottom he's a coward."

"He lost an arm in combat," Dave said.

"And he has a purple heart to prove it." She used that bleak laugh again, and bent to dig cigarettes and a green throwaway lighter from her bag. "But you can buy purple hearts at pawnshops."

Dave went back to the stove, brought the coffeemaker to the table, and poured coffee into the mugs while she lit her cigarette. The smoke smelled good. He found his own cigarettes and lighter lying with his glasses on the folded copy of the morning *Times*. He frowned at the paper. He'd read only the entertainment section this morning, curious about a citywide music festival that yesterday had honored John Cage, whom he'd known long ago. He hadn't read the news—not even the headlines. He picked up the cigarettes, went back to the table, sat down. "When did this killing happen?"

"A little before midnight." She blew smoke away, tasted her coffee. "At the Old Fleet Marina."

Dave stared, the flame of his lighter halfway to his cigarette. "A Vietnamese?"

"Le Van Minh. The man who owns the place."

Dave lit the cigarette and put the lighter down. "I understood he hardly knew where it was."

"If he didn't," she said, "Andy Flanagan told him."

"Flanagan lives there? He's one of the boat people?"

"The one making the most noise," she said. "I don't know that the rest of them agree—they're an odd bunch—but he claims he's their spokesman."

"What did Flanagan do—telephone Le?"

"He wanted a summit meeting." She drank some coffee, turned ash off her cigarette in a big, square clear-glass ashtray. "All he or any of them at the Old Fleet had seen were lawyers handing them vacate notices and deadlines. Andy wanted to talk to the man himself." She gave her head a sorry shake. "He'd once told the others that if Le didn't back down, he'd kill him. Whose country was this, anyway? What had we fought a war for—so a damn Slant could turn Americans out of their homes?"

"I'm surprised Le came. At night? Alone? It's no place for a stranger—not as I remember it."

"Especially not a well-dressed stranger," she said, "driving a large, expensive car. But the lawyers weren't with him. He didn't call them. His son Hai wanted to drive him. But Le wouldn't hear of it. And in a Vietnamese household, the father's word is law."

Dave nodded. "Filial piety," he said. "Obedience. Did he and Flanagan meet?"

"Andy waited on his boat. The appointment was for eleven. And when Le hadn't come on board by midnight, Andy went to ring him again. At the pay phone on the pier. And stumbled over his body."

"Who called the police?"

"Andy, once he'd got over his shock. It's the only

defense he's got. He knew he'd be arrested. But he phoned the police anyway."

"What options did he have?" Dave said. "It would have been stupid to run."

She took a last drag from her cigarette, snubbed it out, blew the smoke away, and gave him a grave and steady look. "Maybe not—not if you won't help him."

"I should have moved to a remote cottage on the Sussex downs and kept bees," he said.

She frowned, tilted her head. "What?"

He sighed. "I'll look into it." Her face lit up, and he lifted a hand. "Abe Greenglass has been my lawyer for a lifetime. He's gotten me out of some very serious scrapes and he's never asked anything of me before, so I'll look into this for you, but that's all. I don't promise to find anything. There may be nothing to find. Flanagan may be slyer than you think."

She shook her head. "He's a lot of things, but sly isn't one of them. You'll find something," she said.

2

The long, narrow wooden walkway creaked under him. A police officer had marked the splintery planks with an outline of Le Van Minh's dead body. Below, in the water, floated yellow ribbon lettered CRIME SCENE . . . BEYOND THIS . . . A yellow- and black-striped sawhorse had fallen over. He looked up. Gulls circled lazily against a clear blue sky. He walked on. The pier swayed. The moored boats fitted no pattern. Among sleek cabin cruisers rocked wooden fishing boats with scaling paint, slim sailing craft with shredded tackle and heaps of mildewed nylon sailcloth, houseboats, kinds of boats he doubted anyone could put a name to.

Along the gangway, scabby steel poles held sagging power lines that stretched to the boats people lived on. He passed a boxy stucco building marked in fading paint RESTROOMS, SHOWERS, warped doors standing half open. A gull swung down and perched on a tilted television aerial atop one of the boats. On the rear deck of this one, a woman with a head of feathery gray hair washed clothes in a square plastic tub. The tub was red and stood on a bench, a box of soap powder and a white bottle of bleach beside it. The woman scrubbed bluejeans on a washboard. Jeans, shirts, underwear hung on a rope above the deck.

Dave called, "May I talk to you?"

She straightened stiffly, rubbed her lower back, winced at him in the noon sunglare off the water. Stocky, ruddy-faced, she was probably seventy. Her voice had a commanding ring to it. "You wait a few days, you can talk to our lawyer. None of us has anything to say to you."

"I'm not from Mr. Le." A gray plank lay across to the boat from the dock. He made to walk aboard.

"Just hold it right there." Wiping her hands on her shirt, she came toward him along a paintless deck, a bulldog set to her jaw. "If you're not from him, you're from the developers, and if you're not from them, you're from the city council." She halted a few feet from Dave. A yellow cat with white markings had been asleep on top of the boat's wheelhouse. Now the cat jumped down and began circling her ankles, bumping, tail straight up. "Well, we're taking up a collection—got nearly five hundred dollars now—to hire an attorney and fight all of you. Lawyers seem to be all anybody understands anymore."

Dave took out the ostrich-hide folder that held his private investigator's license, let it fall open, and held it out arm's length so she could read it if she wanted to across the space of dark water that separated them. She blinked, squinted, shook her head.

"No use. Haven't got my glasses. No point wearing them to wash clothes. They just get steamed up. Or else they fall off into the soapsuds."

"My name is Brandstetter." He slipped the folder back

inside his jacket. "I'm working for the Public Defender handling Andy Flanagan's case. Tracy Davis."

This got her attention. She eyed him, head turned, wary. "Working how?"

He smiled and shrugged. "Ms. Davis doesn't think Andy killed Le Van Minh. She'd like me to find out who did. What do you think?"

She snorted. "What all of us think. That Andy was a fall guy. He'd been raising hell about how they're booting us out of here without a by-your-leave. He was a troublemaker. Powerful people don't like poor people who stand up on their hind legs and fight back."

Dave started to say, "I didn't know anybody liked him," and out in the harbor, beyond the ugly steel lattice-work of the Edward Otis bridge, a freighter blew its whistle, a deep, hoarse roar. The sound shook the place. When the echo died, Dave said, "If I come aboard, it will be easier to talk." She hesitated and he gave her a smile and said, "I think you've got ideas on this that can help me. Help Andy."

She nodded grudgingly. "All right, come on." She turned and walked back aft past the superstructure to the bright tub on its bench. He crossed the plank, jumped down, followed her. He leaned back against a gunwale, and watched her bend over her wash again. She said, "They wouldn't be so crude as to kill Andy outright, would they? A veteran with an arm shot off for his country?"

"So somebody murdered Le to frame him?" Dave said.

She lifted the soaking jeans out of the water, and squeezed suds out of them. She wrung them, grunting with the effort, stretched them flat on a wet patch of deck, took a green plastic garden hose, and sprayed them hard. She flapped them over, sprayed them hard again, turned off the hose, hung the jeans on the rope line, turned to face Dave.

"That's what I think," she said. "I may look crazy, but my brains still work. I taught school till they made me retire. I live on Social Security and a laughable pension. But I live by the ocean, which is what I longed to do all my life and never could." She glanced around at the shabby hulks, the weathered oil derricks, the deserted factories. "It's not Monte Carlo. But I like it, and I want to stay here till I die."

Dave took out cigarettes and lighter, held them up, brows raised. She gave him a nod.

"Go ahead and smoke. I'm not one of those people who enjoys spoiling everybody else's fun. Too much of that these days." She turned back to start rubbing a soggy print dress on the washboard. Dave lit a cigarette. The sea breeze snatched the smoke. Grunting between the words, she said, "They claim it's your health they're interested in, but the truth is, they just want you to be miserable. It's the only way some people can be happy. Like the ones that want me and the rest of us out of here."

"How many of you are there?" Dave said.

"Ninety." She began to wring the dress out. "On forty boats. Couples—old a lot of 'em. But there are youngsters, too, with babies and toddlers." She flapped the dress down on the deck, turned on the hose and rinsed it the way she'd rinsed the jeans. The water ran into the scuppers. Over the hiss and splash of the hose, she went on talking. "You must be good at your work—the way you dress, that car you drive. I saw you park up there." She jerked her head at the seawall.

"Was Le killed just so Andy would be arrested for his murder?" Dave said. "Or do you think whoever did it wanted Le out of the way too?"

"I wouldn't be surprised." She turned off the hose, threw it aside, peeled the dress off the curved deck planks, flapped it over the rope. "Le annoyed the developers and the politicians. He was slow to do what they wanted. He was supposed to have cleared us out of here months ago." She lifted the washboard from the tub, leaned it against the bench and, getting red in the face. picked up the tub, hauled it to the rail, dumped the soapy water overboard. "That was why Andy thought maybe Le was worth talking to."

"Even though he was Vietnamese?" Dave said.

"He didn't like that, but what choice did he have?" She hung the tub on a spike in the wall of the cabin. Hands on hips, she regarded the wash on the line. "Well, that's over for the week." She gave a satisfied nod, turned to him, said, "You feel like iced tea?" She moved off. "Come on inside. Sun's hot."

She opened a little pair of slatted red doors and ducked down a narrow companionway. Dave tossed his cigarette into the water and dropped after her into a dim cabin with threadbare cushions on built-in benches, storage cabinets above, small stove and refrigerator in a corner. Old television set. Pots of geraniums. Books and magazines lay around. Framed photographs hung on the bulkheads, family, friends, a long-ago cocker spaniel. Small, tarnished trophies stood with bric-à-brac on shelves. He put on his glasses and read the engraving on a trophy. Her class had won a state-wide spelling bee in 1939.

The woodwork of the cabin was white with red trim. The white had gone yellow long ago, and the red had dulled and faded. Water lapped the wooden sides of the old craft. It rocked gently, so that the brass lamp overhead swung from its hook in a crossbeam. She told him to sit down, and she banged ice cubes out of a metal tray, dropped them into mismatched glasses, poured tea over them from a chilled glass pitcher with a nick in its rim. She handed him a glass and sat down opposite him.

"It's sugared and lemoned to start with," she said.

"Thanks." Dave tasted it. The best that could be said for it was that it was cold and wet. "Killing sounds a little extreme to me as negotiating practice in a business deal. Framing a fractious tenant for murder isn't common, either."

"You're the expert," she said. "But feelings were raw around here, on both sides. Still are. Most of us simply have no place to go. The Old Fleet was a last refuge. We're desperate. We're digging in our heels. And sometimes men used to having their way lose patience." She drank some of the tea and made a face. "Tastes stale, doesn't it? I guess something in that icebox ought to be thrown out."

"Tracy Davis says Andy has a short temper," Dave said. "Why didn't he do it?"

"He was a talker." She snorted. "All noise. Nobody around here listened to him. We learned to get out of his way when we saw him coming."

"Then how did he end up spokesman for all of you?"

She gave a short, mirthless laugh. "By default, mostly. Not many people like stepping out in front of the crowd."

"You included, Ms.—?" He waited for her name.

"Potter," she said. "Norma. No, not me included. You know that already." Her smile was wry. "But I'm a woman and I'm old. Being either one in this society is a handicap. And up against a gigantic land development outfit, backed up by a bunch of cold-hearted bureaucrats—no, no. We needed somebody with an advantage, a wounded veteran."

"Willing to step out in front of the crowd," Dave said. "Willing to talk."

"Willing and eager." She grimaced. "Nonstop. But we soon saw it wasn't going to help. That's why a few of us pushed for hiring a lawyer. It hurt Andy's feelings, I guess. That was why he phoned Le on the quiet, and asked him to come down here and talk with him, thrash things out between them."

"It never got to that," Dave said, "if Flanagan's telling the truth. He found Le dead on the dock."

She shuddered. "I wish it hadn't happened." She turned her head to look out one of the small cabin windows. "You don't like ugly things happening where you live. This was a peaceful, pleasant place. Out of the world's way. Now . . . it makes you feel naked, vulnerable, nobody to protect you. All sole alone." She turned back. "Makes you angry too, ready to shoot somebody, yourself. It's a feeling I don't like. It's not civilized."

"You didn't hear the shot? The police report says no one heard it, but Tracy Davis thinks that's unlikely. She wonders why people would lie about that. You know these people. Would they? Why?"

"Probably not lying. They're old and go to bed early, or they're young and go to bed early, knowing the kids will get them up at the crack of dawn. There's a few alcoholics that sit up late with their bottles, and a few people dying that sit up late with their pain. But most of us, up that late, would be running the television, wouldn't we? I would. I do. Reading by lamplight's hard on my eyes. I wish it weren't. TV doesn't have much to offer anybody accustomed to a lifetime's reading. But I make do with it. For company."

"It wouldn't have been a loud report," Dave said. "It was only a twenty-two pistol."

She gave a jerk and stared. "A twenty-two pistol?

But—but how could that kill anybody?" She seemed upset. "When I was a girl my brothers had a twenty-two rifle, and it would kill a rabbit or a prairie chicken. But a grown man?" Her tone scoffed, but her eyes were worried. Why? What about?

"It happens. Maybe somebody did hear the shot, looked out, saw something, or someone—and they're afraid to tell the police about it? Has any of you been threatened? Maybe people are afraid their children will be harmed."

"No, there's been nothing like that. Only some heated language from our side—mostly Andy Flanagan's." She gave a snort of laughter. "And if Andy had been threatened, we'd have heard about it, believe me."

"What about the others?" Dave finished off the bad tea. "If they were afraid to tell the police, maybe they told their neighbors." He got to his feet, carried his glass to the galley, set it in the sink. "Maybe they told you."

She eyed him watchfully. "Why me, especially?"

He smiled. "That's how you impress me, as someone people confide in—younger people, especially."

"The old," she said grimly, "have nothing left to confide. All their confidences have gone to the grave with their friends. It's why they can't make new ones."

Dave stood over her, head bowed a little because the ceiling of the cabin was low, and he looked down at her steadily, until she was ready to leave her bitter reverie to draw breath and speak again. The glass was still in her hand. She looked at it surprised for a second. "That's terrible tea," she said. "You shouldn't have had to drink it." She rose and went into the galley. "A person gets out of the way of having company." She poured the tea from her glass into the sink, and peered into the little refrigerator. "I'm afraid there's nothing else here."

"It's all right, thanks," Dave said. "Who told you they heard the shot that killed Le, Ms. Potter?"

She turned sharply. "What did I say? Did I say anyone told me?" She wasn't angry. She was afraid she'd had a memory lapse, had spoken and already forgotten. "I didn't, did I? Am I losing my mind? Nothing frightens me about getting old the way that does."

"You didn't say anyone told you. I just figured someone did. And I figured right, didn't I?"

Her ruddy face closed. "He has reason to be afraid."

"Why? Did the murderer see him?"

She shut the refrigerator door behind her, and came back to him. She'd been shaken for a few minutes here, by his questions, by her memories. Now she was once again stalwart, sure of herself, as he'd found her up on the deck in the sunlight, and as children must have found her in schoolrooms now no more than memories. She faced him calmly, faded blue eyes unwavering.

"I'm sorry, I can't tell you. It was a confidence."

"It wasn't Andy Flanagan he saw," Dave said.

She shook her head.

"Then his testimony could free Flanagan," Dave said. "You understand that, don't you?"

"I'm not sure Cot—" She closed her mouth hard on the half-spoken name. Her smile was wry. "Let me put it this way. I told you most of us tried to avoid Andy Flanagan, but there were some of us Andy made it a point to avoid."

He studied her. "Are you giving me a clue?"

She chuckled. "I knew you'd understand."

3

Up on the deck in the sun and breeze again, he looked for the cat, who had gone back to the cabin roof. He reached up and stroked its fur. He liked cats, but it had been a long time since one had made a home with him. Tatiana had been her name. He frowned to himself—when was he thinking about? The 1940s. She'd delivered a batch of kittens at the foot of the bed one Eastern morning. That fancy white wickerwork bed he'd shared with Rod Fleming, both men in their early twenties. Tatiana was long since dead. So was Rod. Strange. It didn't seem like any time at all.

Tatiana had worn plushy gray and white stripes. Norma Potter's cream and marmalade cat began to purr now, under his hand. He scratched its ears. It closed its eyes in bliss and kneaded the tough weathered roofing with its front paws. "A soft life around here, isn't it?" he said. "All the fresh fish you can eat?" He hadn't kept a cat, of course, because his work had taken him away from home too much. That wasn't fair to an animal.

Wondering how Cecil felt about cats, Dave crossed the boarding plank to the dock and headed for the next boat fed by sagging power lines.

It was a broad, shallow-draft houseboat. Metal. The kind that loaf around the Sacramento delta. How had it got down here? They weren't built for life on the bounding main. This one showed rust at its rivets. On the roof, a young blond man lay on the faded orange canvas webbing of a tubular deck chair. He wore only swim trunks and sunglasses. Nearby, a tattered Hawaiian shirt hung over a corroded railing and flapped in the breeze. Dave called:

"Hello, on board the *Wanderer*."

The young man sat up. Dave winced. Long angry red scars in which the stitching showed marked the young man's belly. His arms and legs were sticks, his ribs stuck out. He took off the sunglasses and squinted. "What do you want?"

"I'm helping with Andy Flanagan's defense," Dave said.

"The stupid son of a bitch is going to need all the help he can get." Delicately running fingers over his marred belly, the young man pondered Dave, trying to make up his mind. At last, he nodded. "Okay. Come on." He reached to snag the shirt and put it on, moving as if he hurt. "On your way, will you duck inside and ask my wife for another soda, please?"

Sea salt had pitted the chrome on the railings of the main deck. He crawled between these. His feet gonged the plating of the deck. The door to the living quarters stood open. He rapped the tin doorframe and poked his head inside. On a sink counter, a young woman with short reddish hair, was changing a baby's diaper. She wore a large man's shirt with long tails. She called, "Just a minute," clipped shut a last safety pin, picked up the baby with a laugh, laid it in a bassinet. She crouched to retrieve a soiled diaper from the floor and, wrinkling her nose, carried this past Dave, to a round metal receptacle on the deck, pulled off the lid, dropped the diaper in, replaced the lid. She turned Dave a half smile. "Did I hear the captain order grog?"

He touched the brim of his canvas hat. "Yes, ma'am."

She went back inside, a refrigerator door sucked open, thumped closed, she brought two icy green cans, and looked somber as she put them into his hands. "Don't stay too long," she said. "He's weak and everything tires him."

"I'll make it quick," Dave promised.

"I wanted him to nap." She looked reproachful. "He can't sleep at night. He lies awake and worries."

There was a ladder to climb. Dave put the cans into jacket pockets and climbed, the effort bringing back a twinge of pain where his shoulder had been knifed by a half-crazy teenager last winter. He reached the roof deck, and stood for a moment, catching his breath. Then he handed the young man on the deck chair one of the cans. He popped the lid, swallowed some of the contents, held out a hand.

"Ralph Mannix," he said. "Who are you?"

Dave shook his hand, spoke his own name, showed his license, said, "You didn't like Flanagan?"

"Hardly knew him. We only came down here six months ago. Last resort, all right?" He made a face. "I've been very sick. Diverticulitis. You know what that is? Your guts develop leaks. Inside. It's a mess. The doctors made it worse. I had to have surgery, and surgery to repair the surgery, and surgery to repair the repairs."

"I saw the scars," Dave said.

"They're only half of it. I owned a delivery service, rush mail, small parcels. It was growing fast. I'd just put in extra phone lines, a computer system. We'd bought a nice place in Westwood—swimming pool, sauna, you name it. When I came out of the hospital the third time, I was stripped. No business, no house, no car, nothing in the bank, and still deep in debt. My wife's folks used their last thousand bucks to buy us this tub. She's got the baby and me to look after, can't go out to work, so she takes in typing here. It's our only income." He turned his face away for a minute, drew a few deep breaths, drank from the green can, worked up a kind of smile. "I'm sorry. I'm alive. That's what counts, isn't it? Where there's life, there's hope." Gloom reclaimed him. "Only now we're going to be chased out of here, and where will we go?"

"You blame Flanagan?" Dave said.

"The committee chose him because he was vocal," Mannix said. "I'd have chosen Norma Potter. She's got some sense. Flanagan's crazy, if you want the truth."

"Crazy enough to murder Le?" Dave said.

"That's what the police think," Mannix said. "And the way he felt about Vietnamese, maybe they're right."

Out past the bridge, a steel loading crane swung atop its tower. Dave watched its cables lift a freight container into sight. He couldn't see the ship the container came from. Slowly the container spun against the sky. "But you didn't know him long."

"I didn't know him long, and I didn't want to. I don't remember the war. I was only thirteen when it ended. But I guess older people figure he's got a right to be bitter. Some of them, anyway. Some of them say the war wasn't Vietnam's fault. We had no business going in there. I don't know. But it isn't just Vietnamese he hates. He hates the Army for sending him there. Hates the Veterans Administration, hates the government—

doesn't matter it's not the same as it was then. Hates pretty much anybody and everybody."

"Was that why you called him stupid?" Dave said. "Or did you have a particular reason?"

"He arranged to meet Le without telling any of us. We're a committee. We're supposed to vote on these things. He went off half-cocked, trying to prove what a born leader he was, and he wrecked the last chance we had."

The sun beat down. Dave tilted up the soda can at his mouth and drank. "What chance was that?"

"Le really didn't know much about the whole thing. Or care, apparently. He'd been stalling, driving the developers nuts. He didn't seem in any hurry to sell the Old Fleet. He sure as hell wasn't hurting for money. Maybe he'd have listened to our side. Now there's only those damn lawyers of his. Them we've met. We'll get no breaks from them."

"Did you hear the shot that killed Le?"

"We slept over at my in-laws in Long Beach," Mannix said. "I'd been up there yesterday to get checked at the hospital. We only got back"—he read a Timex that looked too heavy for his wasted wrist—"three hours ago." His laugh was dry. "Missed all the excitement, right?"

"Flanagan ever offend you personally?" Dave said.

"He sneered when he saw me on the protest committee. What did I have to worry about? My wife's folks were Jewish. Jews have plenty of money. Deb and I and the baby would be all right. The rest of them here were in real trouble. I was so weak, I could hardly stand up. But if I was myself, I'd have beat the shit out of him, one arm or not."

"Norma Potter thinks he was framed."

Mannix tilted his head, wrinkled his brow, weighed

the idea. "To shut him up? Naw. He was a pain in the ass to the developers and the City Council, but he couldn't really hurt them, could he?"

"Yesterday, when you weren't here, he got your plight onto television and into the newspapers. That kind of story rouses public sympathy, turns them against cold-hearted corporations. Maybe that made them take him seriously."

"You don't honestly believe that." Mannix drank off the rest of the soda and set the green can on the deck, wincing when the motion pulled at his scars. "Norma reads too many detective stories. Why wasn't Le just mugged?"

"There was over six thousand dollars in his pockets."

"Well, that lets me out as a suspect." Mannix gave a tired laugh. "I'd have taken the money. Believe it." He went quiet. Dave frowned at the skeletal form stretched out on the flimsy deck chair. He thought Mannix's eyes were closed behind those dark lenses. But his lips moved, he spoke, a whisper. "No—Flanagan just went off his rocker at last." He sighed. "That's all."

"I guess not. Someone here saw the killer." Dave bent to pick up Mannix's empty soda can from the deck. He pushed it into a pocket, his own into the opposite pocket. "He told Norma Potter. He didn't happen to tell you too, did he?"

Maybe Mannix was asleep. Maybe he was only shamming. Whatever the case, he didn't answer. And Dave climbed down the steel ladder and went to the open cabin door to hand in the cans. "Thank you," Mannix's wife said with that pale half-smile of hers. "Each one is worth a penny."

He lit a cigarette, and started along the dock, looking for the next boat wired to a power pole. Movement caught his eye. Maybe thirty yards ahead. He stopped and stood, waiting for whatever it was to show itself again. It was quiet. Water lapped the pier stakes. The whine of the engine that powered the loading crane came to him. Nearer by, gulls cried their creaking cries. A dog, shut up on one of the boats, yelped to get out. Somewhere he heard the muffled quarrelling of soap-opera actors.

Then he saw again what he thought he'd seen before, but hadn't believed. A face, half black and half chalk white, flickered into sight and out of sight on a boat far down the row. Panic was in the eyes that looked at him out of that face. He threw his cigarette into the water, and used long strides to get him to that boat. It was a slim, white, forty-foot sailing craft that hadn't sailed in a long time. STARLADY was painted on its bow.

He didn't ask permission. He swung aboard. Lithe-ness had left his lean body some years back. He knew that, but at moments like this, mind on his work, he forgot. He damn near fell into the water. Hitting the deck, he sprawled. And a tall, running figure tripped over him, scrambled up, and tried to swing over the side to the dock. Dave grabbed one of his long, lean legs.

"Let go." The leg tugged. "I have to go to work."

Dave climbed to his feet, changing his grip from the leg to an arm in a floppy jacket. Under the jacket, the torso was half black, half chalk white. To match the face. So were the leotards. "To work where—Merrill Lynch?"

"Oh, funny. The Arts Festival, man. Crowds down-town, looking to have a good time. I'm a mime, a juggler, a street performer. If I make people laugh, they throw me money."

"Here's money." Dave took out his wallet, slipped a twenty-dollar bill from it. "And you don't have to make me laugh. Just tell me who you saw last night on the dock at eleven. And I don't mean Andy Flanagan."

"Keep your money." His eyes were fixed on the bill Dave held in front of them. He spoke the words faintly. "I don't know nothing about that." He moved to go away again. Dave caught him, pushed the bill into a pocket of the floppy jacket. The young man shook his head hard. "I mean it. I never saw nobody." He waved an arm. "It happened way up the dock, there. How could I see from here?"

"I guess you weren't here," Dave said. "I guess you reached the Old Fleet on the last possible bus from the music center in L.A. You walked to the pier and saw what you saw. And it scared you so you ran and hid. Which is why the police missed you when they questioned everyone else here. But you couldn't keep it to yourself. You had to tell somebody. And that somebody was Norma Potter."

The painted head shook hard. But the eyes were brighter than ever with fear. "No way did I tell her. How could I tell her? I didn't see nothing. Nobody. I swear it to you. Look, I have to go. It will be dark before I get to UCLA. That's all to hell and gone."

"Hell and gone is where you'll end up, telling lies that can send your neighbor to the gas chamber."

"Don't talk theology to me," the painted head said. "I am not some rag-head Baptist nigger. I am an artist and an intellectual. I am a secular humorist, and proud of it." He paused. "Who are you, anyway?"

Dave showed his license and told him why Tracy Davis had hired him. "Andy Flanagan hated a lot of people and a lot of things. And you were among them, isn't that right? He didn't like having you for a neighbor. He avoided you. Because you're black."

"And gay," the painted head said. "Don't ask me to feel

sorry for that pig-track Irish Catholic bigot. I hope they gas him up the ass and hold a match to his mouth." He pulled the twenty-dollar bill out of his pocket and pushed it back at Dave. "Here's your money. I'm going now." He turned away, swung a leg over the side.

Dave caught his jacket. "Wait a minute. Cecil Harris. Does that name mean anything to you?"

"The lovely, tall brother with the smile?" The painted head turned and cocked an eyebrow. "On the Channel 3 news? I never met him." Eyelids batted coquettishly. "But I sure would adore to." He grinned.

"Good. He's a friend of mine, and I think he'd adore to meet you too," Dave said. "You'd make a great story for him. The Old Fleet is news, right now—"

"That filthy rich old chino throwing us out. I'm glad he's dead." He snorted. "Looks like Flanagan was good for something in this world, after all, wasn't he?"

Dave finished his thought: "—and what you do for a living is off-beat, interesting, and a tie-in with the Arts Festival, which is also news right now."

Paint-head's eyes narrowed. "He'd put me on TV, doing my act? You jiving me, Mr. Brooks Brothers?"

"That could change your life, couldn't it?" Dave said. "Where will he find you tonight? What's your name?"

"Carlton Simes," paint-head said. "Cotton, to my friends. There's a big event at Royce Hall. I'll be on the steps—the long, broad steps, you know, ones that face West? But I'll only be juggling tennis balls. Wouldn't dare try cups and saucers tonight." Cotton jumped lightly over the rail onto the dock. "If that sexy Cecil Harris really did show up, the breakage would be terrible."

Dave lay in bed on the sleeping loft in the dark, gazing up at the skylight. The long rectangles of glass were strewn with leaves. Between the leaves stars shone. The red LED numbers of the bedside clock said one forty-nine. The phone hadn't rung. Where was Cecil? Dave had stared hard at the eleven o'clock news on the big television set in the front building, smoking too much, drinking too fast, worried that Cotton Simes wouldn't get his fifteen seconds of celebrity. Cecil had resented the whole thing, grumbled there was no way he'd ever get the piece past the news director. The story at the Old Fleet was murder, not mime.

"There's a link," Dave said, "and when he discovers that later on, he'll be pleased as hell. He'll give you a raise."

But when Dave had left the station, he wasn't sure Cecil would even try. He hadn't just tried. He'd used ingenuity, steered clear of Le's killing, slighted the boaties' protest, used stock teasers of Arts Festival events, shots of other street artists playing instruments, singing, eating fire, then sinuous Cotton doing his sly, mocking mime act on the lamplit, tree-shadowed steps at UCLA. It was the last piece on the show. On a night when news seemed in short supply, the artistry of Cotton Simes been given a generous twelve solo seconds. It was in rotten taste, on the air only because of a vicious murder, but would anybody notice? On a television newscast? Dave doubted it.

Now he heard Cecil's van jounce down from Horse-shoe Canyon Trail into the brick yard, listened for the door slam, the crunching of Cecil's feet across the dry leaves of the courtyard, the turning of the front door lock. A lamp was switched on below. The bathroom door opened and closed. The toilet flushed, water ran. The bathroom door opened. Glass rattled softly at the bar. Dave got out of bed, flapped into a blue corduroy robe,

went down the raw pine stairs. Cecil looked at him from
the shadows of the bar.

"You have a lot to answer for," he said. "When he told
you he'd adore to meet me, 'meet' was not half of what
he meant." Cecil smiled wanly, and gave his head a
wondering shake. "I almost ended up face down in a
bunk. That willowy queen is a demon lover. No way was
I going to get away from him. Not without knocking him
upside the head. Luckily for both of us, his lady came
home."

"Damn," Dave said. "You mean you didn't get out of
him what he'd seen on the dock when Le was killed?"

"I got it." Cecil handed Dave brandy in a big snifter.
"That's how I almost ended up a victim of sexual assault.
I didn't really promise anything"—carrying his own
brandy, Cecil wandered toward the stairs—"but I let him
hope, didn't I? Driving him home to the Old Fleet." He
climbed the stairs as if his feet were heavy. "It's not his
boat. It's hers. She's Lindy Willard, you know, the jazz
singer? Working the Vine Street right now. Cotton is her
fancy man. And from the way he let go of me when he
heard her coming, she doesn't know he's gay, and if she
did, he'd be out on his adorable butt." On the loft, a
lamp lit up.

Dave switched off the lamp below, and climbed the
steps. "That's all very interesting, but what did he tell
you about Le's killers?"

"It's a good time for him right now"—Cecil's voice
came muffled by the shirt he was pulling off over his
head—"because of the Festival, he works every day. But
most of the year, it's only weekends—at the art museum
or the music center." Dave reached the loft. Cecil was
sitting on the far side of the bed, long back bent so he
could unlace and pull off his shoes. He stood and
stripped down jeans and briefs, tossed them on a chair.

"So he's not an artist all the time." Cecil went naked to a stereo rig under the roof slope, rattled brittle boxes, dropped a cassette into the deck, poked steel buttons. Drums bumped. Miles Davis began to play "Tutu." Cecil turned back, smiled, said, "Sometimes he's a busboy." He stretched out on the bed. "And that's where our story begins." He turned on his side. "Come on, I'll whisper it in your ear."

Dave shed the blue robe, laid it over the loft railing, switched off the lamp, and lay down beside Cecil, who put an arm across him. "Tell me," Dave said.

"He had a job at Hoang Pho, a waterfront restaurant down there—and about ten-thirty, when there was nobody left but four Vietnamese men in business suits at a rear table, all of a sudden, the door bursts open and in come these two little guys in black jeans and black T-shirts, right? Black handkerchiefs tied over their faces."

"I remember reading about it," Dave said. "They were armed with Uzis, weren't they?"

"With which they massacred the four men at the table in two seconds flat and were out of there."

"Never to be seen or heard of again," Dave said.

"You got it," Cecil said. "And Cotton was dishwasher there that night. Only person left. The men had paid their check. He didn't have anything to do but wait till they got finished with their conference, and lock up after them. He was in the kitchen, reading *Rolling Stone*, when he heard the shooting. He ran out the back and buried himself in a trash module. Well, they came out the same way, ran right past him. He damn near died of fright. But he peeked out. Getting into their car, they pulled off those handkerchiefs. Light was bad back there, but he saw their faces. And it took him a long time to get over the idea that they'd seen his. The police questioned him, of course, but he didn't tell them."

Miles Davis played a comic riff—"put your little foot, put your little foot, put your little foot right out." Dave said, "And then he came home night before last, and here were these same two little men in black shirts and jeans again, running away from the Old Fleet dock, right?"

"Uh-huh—you guessed it."

"Asians, right?" Dave said.

"'Tough little doll-boys,' he calls them," Cecil said. "'Pretty as poison.'" Cecil lay quiet while "Full Nelson" thumped and tooted jokily around them. When the tune had pranced off into silence, he said, "What's going to happen to Cotton when this comes out?"

"I'll try not to let it come out," Dave said.

"How can you help it? I know you. You think it was a Vietnamese thing, now. Nothing to do with Andy Flanagan. You'll go after the doll-boys, and they'll figure out it was Cotton who tipped you. And he'll be black and white and dead all over. You were going to quit. Why didn't you?"

"I'll protect Cotton," Dave said. "Do you have contacts inside the Vietnamese community?"

"Nobody has contacts inside the Vietnamese community. It can't be done or the police would have done it, wouldn't they?"

"It can be done," Dave said.

4

Hoang Pho. The place made no sense as a setting for murder. It was too bright. From ceiling banks of fluorescent tubes light glared off pale-peach-color walls, off apricot-color formica table tops, off the chrome plate of cane-seated chairs. It gleamed on the triple-gloss coating of the stiff menu card, and made him blink. He dug out his reading glasses, fumbled them on, and the print cleared for him. The meaning of the words did not. *Bun & Mi. Che & Thuc Uong.* He'd read this morning that some missionary had converted the ideograms of ancient Vietnamese into Western phonetics a hundred fifty years ago. If this had helped anyone at the time, it didn't help Dave now.

The tiny young woman poised at his elbow, waiting for his order, understood English no better than he understood Vietnamese, though she nodded, smiled, even tinkled a merry laugh at his questions. He looked around. The crowd of customers in the shiny place was all Vietnamese, none of them speaking English to each other over lunch. He'd have to do without a translator. He sighed, peered again at the menu, and read off to the young woman the name of one dish from under each of the main headings. He'd never liked surprises, but there had to be a first time for everything.

He held the sleek card up for her, and pointed to a listing under *Pho*. "*Cha gio*," he said. "Please." Under *Bun & Mi*, he pointed to and spoke the mysterious words, "*Banh uot thit nuong*," hoping that, whatever they meant, it tasted as good as they sounded. She wrote on a pad, then pointed at another listing, nodding hard, smiling hard, and spoke her only English of the day. "You like, you like." The name of the dish was *bun cha*. From the last section of the card, he chose a dessert whose name he recognized. "*Flan au caramel*," he said. The French had occupied Vietnam for a long time. Had this been their only legacy?

His table was near the window. Waiting, he looked out at the street. It didn't show him much but desertion—boarded-up stores, fading signs, MARINE SUPPLIES, DAY TRIPS, BOAT RENTALS. If he craned to see down the block, one of those warehouses Cecil had described, with most of its windows broken out, loomed against the sky. When he turned and looked the other way, the oil pumps nodded that he'd seen from the Old Fleet Marina. The rent here would be cheap. Or maybe free. Did the tiny exotic waitresses, the almost equally tiny waiters and busboys in some way owe their outlandish presence in this backwater of American urban decay to Le Van Minh who, when he lived, had owned this stretch of waterfront?

Along with bowls of beansprouts, fresh mint, coriander, chilis, a bowl of steaming *pho* came to him in the hands of one of the boys who had to be brothers or cousins to the girls. It must have been a big Vietnamese family occasion that let Cotton get a job here even late at night. *Pho* was a broth made with spicy beef stock filled with square noodles and meat. It was good, but he ate it without attention. He was frowning over Le's murder. The twenty-two was the reason he hadn't quit. It kept bothering him. If the doll-boys Cotton had seen were the killers, why hadn't they brought their Uzis? As an implement of slaughter nothing was surer than an Uzi. If its size was against it, then the next choice would be a .357 magnum or a nine-millimeter automatic. Professionals didn't use twenty-twos. Worse, Tracy Davis had told him it was a pistol the police lab said the bullet had come from.

Cha gio turned out to be the Vietnamese version of egg rolls. Not a rifle, a pistol. A twenty-two pistol was a target-practice gun. Did anybody hunt even small game with a twenty-two pistol? Let alone large game? Let alone man? It could kill. In Le Van Minh's case it had. But ordinarily it simply wounded. He knew of cases where a twenty-two bullet had bounced off a skull, a shoulder blade, a femur, leaving no more than broken skin or a bruise. A plate of rice rolls replaced the plate he'd emptied of *cha gio*. Through their translucent wrappings he saw tiny shrimp. This bullet had gone in at the base of the skull, and traveled upwards. The mark of the professional? Or simply blind luck?

The waitress who had taken his order brought the dish she'd promised him he'd like. *Ban cha*, a platter of charbroiled pork with spicy carrot sauce, noodles, pickled vegetables. He liked it, but again ate it absentmindedly. Were the murders back there, in that cheerfully lighted corner where a Vietnamese grandfather, a young couple, and two little girls laughed and chattered over tall goblets filled with what looked like multicolored jello—were those murders somehow connected to the murder of Le Van Minh? Plainly, this was an area dense with Vietnamese. The restaurant wouldn't be this busy if it had to draw from afar. So, that the killings had happened near each other on the map might mean nothing. He worked on his plate of succulent pork.

He'd stopped in at the *Times* building this morning and read the accounts of the shooting of the four businessmen here that night weeks ago. Two had been importers. Like Le. A third sold industrial properties. The fourth was a funeral director. No motives for their murders had been discovered. Police asked the cooperation of the Vietnamese community, it was politely promised, but never given. The *Times* said rumors were widespread of an underground terrorist group. But were its roots in the angry divisions between factions in the war-ravaged homeland? Or in illegal immigration, drugs, prostitution, gambling here? No one would say. Dave washed down his *flan* with French iced coffee laced with cream.

His tiny waitress had taken the little tray with the check and his American Express card on it, but a stout, short, moon-faced man brought it back. Dave had noticed him moving among the lunchers, stopping at this table and that, smiling affably, speaking a few words, joking and, when he thought Dave wouldn't notice, studying Dave uneasily. He took a pen from a jacket pocket and handed it to Dave.

"Everything satisfactory?" He spoke English with a French accent. Dave nodded and uncapped the pen and bent to sign the receipt. He handed the pen back with a smile. "Better than satisfactory," he said with a smile, and meant it. He glanced around. "I'm odd man out, though, right? An intruder?"

The man looked shocked and pained. "Not at all. We welcome everyone who enjoys good food."

"Then I'll tell people," Dave said. "This place is a real find." He tilted his head to indicate the shabby street, its shabbier surroundings. "A little unexpected in this district."

The man gestured at the tables, gave a Gallic shrug, a wry smile. "As you see—" He grew somber. "But you may assure your friends, it is quiet here. Entirely safe. One may park on the street, walk on the street without fear."

Dave stood up. "But not sit in that corner." He jerked his head at it. "Not late at night."

The moon face went white. "Shh. M'sieur, please."

"Who did it?" Dave asked. "Who were they? Why?"

The man took Dave's arm and steered him into an alcove. "Who are you?" he hissed. "What kind of questions are these?"

Dave took out the folder and showed the man his license. He told him who he was and who he was working for. "You're near the Old Fleet Marina. That's where Le Van Minh was murdered night before last. You knew him. He owns this building, isn't that right?"

The round head nodded, eyes anxious. "I had met him, yes. It is how I learned of this place."

"And your customers who were killed, Mr. Phat, Mr. Tang, and the others. Did they know him too?"

"Perhaps—I don't know." He gestured helplessly. "But it had nothing to do with me. I am a simple restaurateur, M'sieur. These were wealthy men. I am not of their kind."

"And you have no idea who slammed in here late that night and slaughtered them?"

"No one knows—not even the police."

"Someone does know," Dave said. "Maybe a lot of people know, but they're all too frightened to say. Isn't that how it really is, Mr.—?"

"Hoang Duc Nghi," the short man said, and shook Dave's hand. "People may well be frightened, Mr. Brandstetter. Our world is not your world. In our world for as long as most of us can remember, the nights were filled with terror, and sunrise promised only death. To Americans, violence, bloodshed, torture are for watching on the television." His smile was wan. "Television is the American's world."

"Is that such a bad thing, Mr. Hoang? Compared to living in terror? If your people won't tell the police who these killers are, won't things just get worse?"

Hoang laughed. "The police? What reason have we to trust the police? You don't understand." He put a hand on Dave's arm. Urgently. "Let it alone, Mr. Brandstetter." He glanced nervously out at the room. "We may be being watched right now. If it is known that you are investigating these matters, you may have been followed here. You may be a marked man. If I am seen talking to you, so may I."

"Then you do think there's a connection between Le's murder and the ones that happened here?"

Hoang shook his head desperately. "I never said so."

"Tell me where to start looking," Dave asked him.

"Impossible." Hoang took Dave's elbow, put a friendly arm around him, walked him toward the door. He wore his most affable face, and smiled not only up at Dave, but around at the others in the room, in case any of them were noticing. He opened the street door for Dave, and not quite but almost pushed him out onto the sidewalk. Something tugged at Dave's jacket pocket as he stumbled into the sunlight. The pocket must have caught on the door latch.

"Goodbye, Mr. Brandstetter," Hoang said. "Thank you for coming." Back turned on the diners, so they couldn't see the warning in his eyes, he said the opposite of what he meant: "Come again soon."

"Thank you, Mr. Hoang." Dave smiled, raised a hand in farewell. "I'll do that." He walked along the gritty, cracked, sunstruck sidewalk to his Jaguar. He started the engine and air conditioner, let the brake go, and remembered the pocket. Frowning down, he felt for a tear and didn't find one. But something was in the pocket. It had been empty. The suit had only just come back from the cleaner. He didn't remember putting anything into it. It must have been Hoang. Dave's fingers closed around two smooth little cubes. What? Some Vietnamese equivalent of after-dinner mints? He pulled them out and sat staring at them.

They were a pair of dice.

"He isn't here." Lindy Willard shielded her eyes with a hand. She wore white sailor pants and a bikini top and sat at a metal table atop the superstructure of the dazzling white *Starlady*, eating croissants, drinking what looked like tomato juice. "Who's wanting him?" Her voice was powerful and easy, as it sounded when she sang. But she no longer looked like the Lindy Willard Dave had gone many times to hear at the Melrose Cavern twenty years ago. She'd taken off weight, but it had wasted her instead of making her look younger. Her rusty hair was thin and frazzled. "I've seen you on television, haven't I?" She set down her drink, stood, came to the railing, studied him. "That insurance detective. Brandstetter—that's who you are. Big time. What you want with a little fish like Cotton Simes?" Her glorious voice echoed off the water, off the sea wall. "You mean to tell me those family jewels aren't his?"

Dave laughed. "Can I come aboard?"

"Come have some breakfast. I've got more Bloody

Marys here than are good for me, anyway." Dave
boarded the *Starlady* without falling this time, and
climbed to where she sat at the table again. "Sit down,
please." She pushed toward him a basket of croissants
nestled in a gingham napkin. She poured from a frosty
pitcher, and handed him the glass. "I don't get a lot of
callers. I'm a has-been, you know." She lit a cigarette
and gave a throaty chuckle. "And let me tell you, it's got
its points. For one thing—go ahead, eat, honey—a has-
been don't have to suffer fools gladly."

Dave laughed again. "You haven't tried me yet."

She sobered. "Oh, darlin', you no fool. Those talk
shows sell stupid by the square yard. You get on there,
and it reminds people there's such a thing as a human
brain."

"I have a lot of your recordings," he said.

"Uh-huh, and the gray hair to show for it." The
wonderful laugh came again. But it didn't light her eyes.
They were sad and tired. "Well,"—she drank from her
glass—"it was fun while it lasted." She sighed and this
time the chuckle was mechanical. "Only I thought it
would last forever. I should have saved my money."

"Aren't people coming to the Vine Street these
nights?"

"A few." She waved a hand with long, enamelled nails,
amused, dismissive. "Mostly just to see if it's true I'm
still alive. I sing to a lot of empty tables."

"Why the boat?" Dave said. "Why the Old Fleet
marina?"

"The boat was some record executive's way of paying
me when he went bankrupt. And since I couldn't sail
away to luxurious retirement in Tahiti, I ended up living
on it in the cheapest berth I could find. Now they
putting us out of here, I guess I'll sell it if I can find a fool
to buy it, and move to a rose-covered cottage in Watts."

"Jazz is making a comeback," Dave said. "You'd be welcome anywhere."

She held up both hands in protest. "You sat around airports lately? O'Hare, Kennedy, Dallas, Atlanta? Waiting for planes that never take off? You tried to get comfortable on an airplane, lately? Oh, darlin'—spare these old bones. No way is Lindy Willard going on the road again."

"Make records, then," Dave said.

"What for? They don't sell."

"They'll always sell to me," Dave said.

She laughed and wagged her head. "Oh, baby, I am glad you showed up this morning. My heart was in my shoes." She sighed. "You see, Cotton's left me."

"What do you mean?" Dave frowned and sat forward.

"Packed up and took off." Her face sagged into tired lines. "Said he'd be back. Sometime." Her laugh was bleak. "Sometime never."

"Took off for where?" Dave said.

She eyed him. "What's wrong? He's scared, isn't he? Whimpered in his sleep last night, tossed and turned. I asked him, but oh, no, nothing wrong, just he's overworked is all." She smiled wryly. "Now that is truly a joke."

"Where's he gone?" Dave said.

Her look was guarded. "Why do you want to know?"

"I want to protect him—if I can."

"Gifford Gardens," she said. "His sister. Opal."

"Her last name Simes too?" Dave said.

She nodded. "Schoolteacher—no use for men."

"Who else did he tell where he was going?"

She looked at the greasy water, the seedy boats, the cracked, stained seawall. "Who would he tell around here? Andy Flanagan, the black man's friend?"

"Flanagan's in jail," Dave said. "Cotton wouldn't tell them at Hoang Pho, would he?"

She cocked her head, frowning, eyes narrowed. "How'd you know about Hoang Pho?"

He gave her a thin smile. "It's my job to know."

She sat very still. "Cotton didn't tell you what he saw the night those Asian gentlemen were shot."

"He told that TV reporter who brought him home last night. Traded the information for a spot on the late news."

"Was that child a reporter? Damn. I warned Cotton never to tell nobody. A reporter! God give me strength."

"It was off the record," Dave said, "for my ears only."

"When it's gangsters, first thing you learn in the music business is see no evil, hear no evil, speak no evil."

"He saw them again when Le Van Minh was killed."

She put a hand to her mouth. "Oh, my God."

"Maybe he'll be safe in Gifford Gardens," Dave said.

She said grimly, "From Vietnam terrorists, maybe. Not from his neighbors. Gifford Gardens!" She gave a shudder.

"I'll need the address there," Dave said. "And the phone number, too, please."

She pushed back her chair. "I'll get it for you." She walked toward the ladder. She always walked as if she was sheathed in sequins. "Then I will burn that page of my little black book, and wipe all memory of it from my mind."

5

Gifford Gardens was tract houses on land bulldozed of trees and brush beside a creek. Slapped up out of green lumber to answer a housing shortage after World War II, its builders hadn't told eager buyers how the creek overflowed every winter. It took the county years to line the creekbed with cement slabs to stop the flooding. And by then, nobody much wanted to live there. Gifford Gardens became a slum in the sun and that was what it still was.

Dave had worked on a case out here a few years back. It might have been yesterday. The stores fronting the street that paralleled the creek were still vacant, neon signs broken, paint flaking. Maybe everything was a little bit dingier than when he'd last seen it. But the ragged winos—black, white, latino—seated with their brown-paper-bagged bottles along the curbs, or shuffling down the soiled and trash-blown sidewalks looked no different.

When he was here before, the old Gifford mansion, all

jigsaw-work porches, scalloped shingles, cupolas, had stood on a hill, dominating the place. The last Gifford had still occupied it then, a half-crazy old man, who spied on the town through binoculars from an attic window. Now Dave looked for the mansion, looming up through its untrimmed trees. It was gone. From an intersection where he stopped for a traffic light, he got a clear view of the hill. Banners fluttered off wires above tarmac parked with glossy used cars.

As if joblessness, hunger, and all that went with them weren't enough, gangs kept the town cowering. The Edge were young blacks who roved the streets in rebuilt Mustang cars. The GGs were latinos. Drive-by shootings were common, where grandmothers and little children died as often as gang members. Not the shackiest house was safe from break-ins. No one with sense brought a good car out here. Dave was driving an old pale yellow Valiant, creased along a door and fender by some long ago sideswipe. Kevin Nakamura garaged it for him up in the canyon, the tank full of gas, the engine tuned, but with strict orders never to wash it.

Dave turned it left up Guava Street now. He was wrong. There had been changes. A little prosperity had combined with a lot of despair and householders had bolted steel bars over their windows. They were painted black, and bore stingy ornamentation, but they were there to prevent crime. If you somehow had managed to buy a TV set, maybe you could hang onto it, instead of having it vanish to feed some crack addict's habit. If it meant jailing yourself, too bad. Here was Opal Simes's address.

The house was neatly painted pale green with dark green trim. A big avocado tree bent over the roof. Old ground ivy covered the front yard. A concrete front stoop with wrought-iron railings had pots of begonias standing on it. The effect was peaceful, well-ordered. What spoiled the effect was a ten-foot-high chainlink fence with razor wire on top and a padlock on the gate. A brindle pit bull, heavy in the chest, broad of muzzle and piggy of eye, came around a corner of the house, trotted down the straight strip of walk between the ground ivy, and stood with its nose to the gate wire, looking at him. It didn't bark. It didn't growl. It didn't have to, and it knew it didn't have to.

He drove away, and found a pay phone in a half booth of cracked glass panes clinched in steel. The phone abutted the white painted brick side of a liquor store, just a step from the sidewalk, in a rutted hardpan parking lot. This had once been a hangout for the GGs. Today, at the alley end of the lot, a Mustang sat, its sandpapered doors hanging open, four young blacks inside, leather jackets, dark glasses, cans of beer. He felt them watching him as he put a quarter into the telephone and punched the gritty steel buttons with Opal Simes's number. School would start soon. She should be at home. She was.

He told her his name, and that he was working for the San Pedro County public defender's office on a murder case. "Your brother knows me, and that could make trouble for him—if it hasn't already. I have to reach him right away."

"Carlton?" She acted surprised. "Why, Carlton isn't here. I haven't seen him in weeks. The Arts Festival is on in Los Angeles. He's working. He's an entertainer."

"I've been to the boat where he was living," Dave said. "They told me there he'd gone to your house. He's in danger, Ms. Simes. It's really vital that I talk to him."

"You give me your message," she said. "And if he does come here, I'll pass it on to him."

"Not over the phone," Dave said. "Come to your gate.

I'll show you my identification. We have to talk privately. There's nothing private about a telephone."

She didn't answer but he heard her breathing. "Well—" she said at last, "you sound awfully serious, Mr. Brandstetter. You come over here, and we'll see, all right?"

"Thank you." He hung up the receiver, turned, and the four youths from the Mustang stood around him. From the hand of one hung a tire iron. "Let's see your ID."

"You a police officer?" Dave said.

"Police officers don't come around this part of town. They know better. This our territory. We the Edge, and the Edge be the law here." He held out the hand not burdened with the tire iron. "Ain't nobody come here don't check in with us." He grinned at his friends. "Right?"

A fat one nodded solemnly. "Too right, man."

"And pay their taxes." A scar-faced one leered.

"Fair enough," Dave said, and reached inside his jacket and brought out a Sig Sauer nine-millimeter semi-automatic. Since he'd bought it, more often than not, he'd forgotten to carry it. Today, knowing Gifford Gardens, he'd remembered. He pointed it at the chest of the youth with the tire iron, and jacked a bullet into the chamber. The eyes of the Edge members opened wide. "This is a Swiss army weapon," Dave said. "Capable of shooting eighty thousand rounds without jamming. It's only been fired a few times. So if I were you, I wouldn't count on its jamming now."

Tire-iron snorted. "Look like a plastic toy to me."

Dave bent his knees a little and fired past the kid's ear. The gun bucked, hurt his hand, the noise made his head ring, but the gesture worked. Tire-iron and company broke and ran for the Mustang—stumbling over each other in panic. Dave stepped around the corner of the liquor store, crossed the sidewalk, slammed the door of the old Valiant, and roared off. His heart hammered. He was too old for this. He sped up pointless streets, back-trailed, dodged through trash-strewn alleys, and didn't return the gun to its holster until he had parked in front of Opal Simes's house again and searched side and rear-view mirrors for signs of the Mustang. He tapped the Valiant's wheezy horn, got out of the car, locked it for whatever good that would do, and stood waiting at the gate again, the pit bull looking patiently up at him.

Opal Simes came out the front door carrying a chain leash. She let Dave slide the folder with his license through the narrow space between steel gate frame and steel fence post. She read the license. She studied his face, his clothes. She gave him back the folder, bent, attached the chain to the dog's collar, excused herself, and led the dog away around the corner of the house. When she came back she still held the chain. She was tall and slim, and there was no denying she was Cotton's sister. If in fact she had, as Lindy Willard said, no use for men, it was their loss. She was even more beautiful than Cotton. She used a key on the gate's padlock, opened the gate, looked up and down the street, let him in, relocked the gate, and led him up the walk. "All these precautions must seem bizarre to you."

"Not if my car doesn't seem bizarre to you," he said.

On the stoop, reaching for the door, she turned and looked him up and down. "It doesn't match your clothes." Her smile came and went quickly, as if smiling wasn't something she did often. "Carlton would call those very expensive threads, man."

Dave laughed. "He calls me Mr. Brooks Brothers."

She stuck in a key and opened the door. "Come in." He followed her into a pleasant, quietly furnished living room. With many bookshelves. He smiled glumly to himself about those. Two twenty-five-inch televisions, one a monitor. Two VCRs. Hundreds of video tapes. The room beyond held a computer with a laser printer, and an office-size copying machine. She noticed him looking at all this. "You see the reason for the fence and the dog?" she said. "The school is trashed so often, it seemed better to bring my office home. It's supposed to be a secret, but secrets don't keep when a whole staff has to know. The students are bound to find out, and not all the students love Ms. Simes."

"You're the principal," he said.

"It's a dirty job, but somebody has to do it."

He frowned. "No electronic security system?"

"Our police don't jump to respond," she said. "Too many officers killed. They approach with caution. Time they get to the scene, you're raped, maimed, murdered, or all three, and the ones who did it are gone with your worldly goods in the trunk of their car." She read her watch. "It's almost five." She started toward the rear of the house. "Would you like a glass of white wine?"

"It's not necessary," Dave said. "Your brother knows the faces of two men who have committed four, possibly five murders." She turned back and stared at him. "If you know where I can find him, it's important that you tell me. Getting away from the Old Fleet Marina was a smart move, but if he's still in the L.A. area, he's in danger."

She drew a deep breath, blew it out again, came to him, frowning, disturbed. "You have a card?" Her hand shook as she read it. She took it into the room with all the office equipment, tucked it under a corner of a multi-line telephone. "I'll keep it. If he gets in touch with me, I'll tell him to call you." Troubled, uncertain, she left him.

The neighborhood, the house, were eerily quiet for a place so menaced. Distantly, he heard her speak, and he tensed. But it wasn't Cotton's voice that answered. It was the dog's. Its bark sounded like a bronchial attack. He heard the click of its claws on what was probably kitchen flooring. He sat down, and noticed again something he'd seen when he entered the place but hadn't registered. In a corner. An airline bag. With a white smear on it. He jumped up, strode across, unzipped the bag. Inside were black and white tights, black and white ballet shoes, a black glove, a white glove, five balls, three black, two white, black and white bowling pins, black and white cubes, and a draw-string bag of theatrical makeup. That smear was clown white.

"What are you doing?" Opal Simes held glasses of wine.

"Cotton is here," Dave said. "These things are his."

"Oh, damn. That five-year-old." She set the wine glasses down, snatched up the airline bag, and hurled it across the room. "How can I protect such an irresponsible child?" Tears ran down her face. Not sad tears. Tears of vexation. She brushed at the tears with her fingers, and gave Dave a woeful smile. "I'm sorry. I never was any good at lying. I hate it. But he begged me, and I said I would." Her laugh was self-mocking. "I never could say no to Carlton." She nodded, shamefaced. "Yes. He's here."

Dave moved past here. "Where?"

"Out in the garage. I don't try to keep a car anymore. Stripped so often, stolen so often. I pay a janitor at the school to drive me to work and home. So the garage isn't used. I fitted it out as an apartment for Cotton. It's always here for him."

Dave looked toward the door in the rear wall of the office room. "Where's the dog?"

"In the kitchen, eating his supper." She went to the front door, opened it. "We can go around by the outside." She started out ahead of him.

He caught her arm. "Wait here, please," he said.

She looked down at his hand. She raised her eyes, and alarm was in them. "What are you going to do?"

He smiled and shook his head. "If you knew, you might have to lie about it. To some very unpleasant types. And you're no good at lying, and that could get you killed as well as Cotton. So you'd better not know. Understand?"

"Not really," she said.

Stepping around the begonias, he went past her down the steps. "I'll explain it to you later." He headed for the driveway. "When it's over. When it's safe."

The backyard had grass and a pair of apricot trees, fruit golden among green leaves, branches arched over from the weight of the fruit. He used his knuckles on a side door to the garage. "Cotton, open up. It's Dave Brandstetter."

"Who is the last man on earth," Cotton shouted, "I want to see. Go away. How did you find me, anyhow?"

Dave didn't want to shout. He spoke close to the door. "It was easy, too easy. You're not safe here." He tried the door. It was locked. "Don't you see—if I could find you, they can find you."

There was a rattling on the far side of the door. It opened. Cotton was naked except for a towel. Its whiteness made a gleaming contrast to his sleek bronze skin. He was wet, fresh from a shower. He poked his head outdoors, looked quickly this way, that way. "Who you talking about?"

"The ones you call doll-boys," Dave said.

Cotton grabbed him. "Get in here." He pulled Dave inside and slammed the door. "I am pissed with you." It was a double garage. It still smelled of dripped motor oil, gasoline, exhaust fumes, but it was carpeted, and furnished with two neat armchairs, a coffee table, a bed, a chest of drawers, small sink, small stove, refrigerator. In a corner a door stood open on a tiny bathroom where a mirror over a basin was steamy. Cotton took bikini shorts from the chest of drawers. He shed the towel and pulled the shorts up his long legs. "You send that Cecil Harris around, I tell him stuff you know is worth my life—and then when I want us to get it on together, he's shocked."

"What did you take me for?" Dave said. "A pimp?"

Cotton pulled on an enormous muslin shirt with many pockets. "You said he'd adore to meet me. Isn't that what you said?" He sat on the bed and drew up white crew socks over his long feet. "What was I supposed to make of that?"

"I didn't say he'd sleep with you," Dave said.

"Oh, please, I talk ignorant because it turns women on and makes the master race feel superior. But it didn't fool you." Cotton dragged muslin trousers from a hanger on a nail driven into a stud. "You knew you didn't have to say it. You knew I'd think it." He shook out the trousers and kicked into them. They were roomy enough for two of him. "I wouldn't tell you about the doll-boys and Mr. Le, so you sent a brother, right? A gay brother at that."

"And he gave you what I promised." Dave watched Cotton thread a gaudy necktie through the belt loops, knot it at his narrow waist. "A spot on TV. Didn't you see it?"

"Only the tape when we got to the station." Cotton sat on the bed again, this time to put on Adidas. "Not the newscast. We was on the freeway by then." He bent to lace up the shoes. "If it was only you told me it was on, I wouldn't believe it, but Opal says she saw it, and it was lovely—but Opal, she thinks anything I do on or off TV is lovely." He grew gloomy. "Wish my lady felt like that."

Dave said, "She misses you. She told me so."

"She gets all the loving she need from the folks out in the smoke when she sing." He shook his head. "I shouldn't have told Cecil. Shouldn't have gone on TV. I knew that, soon as the lights was out and my head was on the pillow."

"Lindy said you couldn't sleep."

Cotton said, "It was her that sent you here."

"She'd like you to live." Dave held out a folded paper.

Cotton looked at it as if it were a scorpion, and put his hands behind him. "What's that—more trouble?"

Dave smiled briefly. "I've made you an airline reservation. The name of the airline and the flight number are on there. The ticket is paid for. All you have to do is pick it up and walk aboard. The red-eye for New York. Tonight."

Cotton took the paper, unfolded it, studied it. He frowned at Dave. "I don't know anybody in New York."

"I'm sure you make friends easily," Dave said.

"Where am I going to sleep?"

"I've written the hotel name on there. I've reserved you a room. That also is paid for. Stay there until I tell you it's safe to come back."

"You're going after the doll-boys," Cotton said. "And you think they'll figure out it was me tipped you about them. Them and those men at the Hoang Pho."

"They may not know yet that I'm after them, but they will soon. Don't look so worried. I could be overreacting. You aren't sure they saw you. Maybe they didn't." He used a smile. "Cecil always claims he's invisible in the dark. Why not you?"

He snorted. "I was still painted half white when they came running at me off that pier."

That reminded Dave. "What kind of guns did they have?"

Cotton's forehead wrinkled. He blinked. "Guns. No guns. Not that night. I didn't see no guns."

Dave grinned. "Good." He pushed a fold of bills into the breast pocket of Cotton's blowsy shirt. "Expense money. If you need more, I'll wire it. But don't phone me. Phone Tracy Davis at the San Pedro County district attorney's office. Her name and number are on there."

Cotton peered at the paper again, and checked his watch. "Jesus. LAX. Take me forever to get there from here. My car got repossessed. And Opal sold hers."

"Pack your clothes," Dave said. "I'll drive you—if you don't mind hiding on the floor behind the seat."

Cotton eyed him. "Don't want us seen together, right?"

"If we haven't been already, why take the chance?"

6

Driving that wreck of a car had left him with aches. He edged stiffly between the crowd of candlelit diners at Max Romano's restaurant to his table in the far corner, where Tracy Davis waited for him. He read his watch. Seven fifty-five. The glass she was turning by its stem on the thick white linen tablecloth had half an inch of white wine in it. She had made wreckage of a little loaf of fresh-baked bread, a small plate of salad. She looked up at him with a smile she didn't mean. He dropped wearily into a chair across from hers.

"Airport traffic," he explained. "Sorry."

"Here's the list you asked for." She reached down and got her shoulder bag from the floor beside her chair. "But I'm not sure you want to go on with this." She set the bag in her lap and rummaged inside it.

"No? Why is that?" Dave started to lift a hand to attract attention, and saw Max Romano waddling toward him. For a time, here, Max had been scared onto a diet by doctors, but he was getting fat again. The skeletal Max, beautiful suits hanging off him, had unsettled Dave. He had looked sick, miserable, dying. He was close to eighty. Maybe he was sicker now and in more danger, but he looked splendid, his sleek old happy self. His gold teeth glittered, and the diamonds on his rings sparkled. He'd had to store the rings while he starved himself. They kept falling off. Now they were held securely in place by pudgy flesh again. He set a big squat glass down in front of Dave. Glenlivet over ice.

"You were going to retire," he said. "It doesn't seem to agree with you. You look pale, my friend."

Dave worked up a smile for him. He nodded at Tracy Davis. "This young lady talked me out of quitting. Tracy Davis, Max Romano. Max and I go back forty years. Ms. Davis is a public defender."

Max shook her hand and gave her a smile but he didn't smile at Dave. He looked gravely disappointed, and shook his head, where now only a few thin strands of once glorious hair lay across a bald scalp. "I would have hoped at least it was not a dangerous case. But you are carrying a gun."

"To make it less dangerous," Dave said. "Swordfish in the kitchen tonight, Max?"

Max nodded. "And for the young lady?"

She laughed. "I thought you'd never ask." She eyed the menu through those green-rimmed glasses for only a moment, handed Max the menu, and said, "The same, please."

"Vichyssoise to start?" Dave asked her.

"Sounds marvelous," she said. "But I don't deserve it."

Max said. "You shall have it, anyway," and left them. It was good to see him walk briskly again. When he was thin, he'd moved slowly, feet dragging, shoulders slumped. Their waiter's name was Avram. He'd come to work here from Israel—it seemed like only yesterday. He'd been a boy. Dave was shocked to see gray in his hair now, as he brought fresh bread, spinach salad for Dave, and filled Tracy Davis's glass with wine again.

Dave drank some of the good scotch, shut his eyes, let the whisky start reviving him, then lit a cigarette and gave Tracy Davis an inquiring frown. "Why won't you deserve it? Why won't I want to go on with the case."

Glass to her mouth, she gave a brief laugh with regret in it. "Because you're going to think even less of my client now than you did before. Andy wasn't wounded in combat. He got caught in a barroom brawl in Saigon, and fell on a broken bottle, trying to escape. He cut his arm badly, was afraid of the MPs, and tried to take care of it himself. Infection set in, and by the time medics saw it, it couldn't be saved."

"You didn't mislead me," Dave said. "You told me he was a coward."

She sawed glumly at the little loaf on its wooden board. "I could have done without glaring proof."

"It doesn't change anything," Dave said. "Whatever his drawbacks, Andy Flanagan didn't kill Le Van Minh. Not the way things are adding up." He put out his cigarette, worked on his salad, told her about his day. Her eyes were wide. "I see now why you wanted this." She handed him the folded paper she'd got from her bag. "I don't know how complete it is. It's mostly guesswork, to be honest. The police suspect this place and that, but when they raid, they're always too late. They can't get informers into the Vietnamese community but they can't help think the Vietnamese have informers in the police department."

Dave watched Avram set before them bowls of creamy soup cradled in crushed ice. "No Vietnamese officers?"

She shook her head. "That's what's so baffling."

Dave reached across for the list, put on his reading glasses, read the names and addresses, folded the paper again, and tucked it into an inside jacket pocket. He put the glasses away, and gave her a smile. "It's a start," he said. "Thanks for your trouble."

"You're the one who's gone to all the trouble." She picked up a spoon and tasted her vichyssoise. "Heavenly," she said. She tilted her head, looked at him doubtfully. "Lindy Willard? Honestly? I thought she was dead."

"She's alive." Dave tried his soup. "Cotton leaving her bed when he did may keep her that way. But I hope she finds a buyer for the *Starlady* tomorrow, and clears out."

"She could go to New York too, couldn't she?" Tracy Davis said. "Sing in nightclubs there?"

"She's taken against flying," Dave said.

Mel Fleischer opened the door himself. It was a heavy carved door of pale reddish wood, with black, hand-forged hardware. Fleischer was sixty-five, a successful banker. Once lean and patrician, he was jowly now and paunchy. He and Dave were of an age, but the years were treating Dave differently—turning him reedy and brittle. Dave's friendship with Mel dated back to high school. A horizontal friendship, fumbling and funny to remember, but the affection had been real and had never waned.

Mel's house crowned a ridge near the HOLLYWOOD sign in the hills overlooking the city. The house was 1920s Mediterranean, thick chalky-white walls, red tile roofing, a round tower for a circular staircase of glazed painted tiles, unmistakeably California. Nothing else would do for Mel Fleischer. California was the true love of his life. He collected paintings by California artists.

Some of the young ones he helped with money. He sat on the board of the L.A. County Museum, and owned shares in galleries along La Cienega Boulevard and in Beverly Hills.

"Dave, good. I'm glad you're early." He enclosed Dave in a bear hug, and led him out of the circular entry hall down terra cotta tile steps into a vast living room. "I can't think how long it's been since you were here." Thick black rough-hewn beams crossed overhead beneath a pitched roof. Against the white walls hung big handsome paintings, brown hills under wide skies; horses in long, sloping meadows, mountains in the background; the rickety trellis of the old Angel's Flight tramway in Downtown L.A.—each picture carefully lighted. But Mel had left space for bookshelves, all the same. Dave smiled to himself again.

"Too long," Mel said. "Sit down, sit down." He waved a graceful hand, and started off down the long room. He was genuine and funny, but there'd always been something queenly about his bearing, a hint of the Ronald Firbank cardinal. The ragbag look of his fashionably loose slacks, broad-shouldered blouse didn't change that. Dave grinned. Mel called back, "Makoto's still in the shower. What will you drink to pass the time until he makes his spectacular entrance?"

"Brandy, please." Dave sat on a seventeenth-century chair, all black lathe-turned wood and gold-shot red brocade, complete with fringe. "It's generous of you to lend him to me for a night. It's good of him to take the time."

"He's happy not to have to be reading student essays on *The Imaginary Invalid*." Glassware chimed in the shadowy distance. "He says they're no better than they were five years ago. And very little different. Sometimes I find him staring at the printouts that list his students.

Looking for familiar names. He's sure those who sat in his classes long ago have in some mysterious way come round again." Mel handed Dave brandy in a snifter. He dropped onto a couch of the same style as Dave's chair, lifted his own glass, smiled. "Here's to old times." He tasted the brandy, and looked wounded in his feelings. "You might have brought me Cecil to help pass the lonely night."

"He's working, and if he wasn't, he'd insist on going with Makoto and me. What's wrong?"

An imperious finger pointed. "You're wearing a gun." Mel looked severe. "You didn't say this would be dangerous."

"It won't be." Dave stood, shed his jacket, unbuckled the holster, handed it to Mel. "Here, you keep the gun." He put his jacket on again. "I'm happy to be rid of it."

The gun horrified Mel. He dropped it on the couch. A step sounded on the stairs. The circular tower echoed. Mel turned to the short, muscular young man who came in, "Don't you know my dear old friend here is insanely reckless? He's nearly gotten himself killed a dozen times. Makoto, I refuse to let you leave this house with him."

"Relax," Makoto said, "it's only for a couple of hours. All we're going to do is lose a little of Dave's money." When Dave had met him, ten years back, Makoto's English, learned in a Japanese classroom, had been hard to understand. Now there wasn't a flaw in it. He'd been a college student then. Now he was an instructor, teaching French literature. His passion at that time had been rollerskating, and he had dressed for it. Now he wore a dark suit and tie, dark shoes, very conservative. He came back into the lamplight, carrying a drink. He asked Dave, "Do I look okay?"

"Just right," Dave said. "If no one tries to strike up a conversation with you in Vietnamese, you'll be perfect."

"I'll zap 'em with French." Makoto leaned by a rounded, adobe-style fireplace, and sipped his Coke. "Vietnamese speak French. At least, they used to."

"We'll hope we don't have to lean on that," Dave said. "But it's nice to have it. In case."

Mel said fretfully, "I just don't understand this at all. Dave, what are you up to? You were going to retire. Now here you are plunging into murky opium dens in search of the infamous Dr. Fu Manchu. Will you never grow up?"

"Thanks for the brandy." Dave rose and gave Mel's shoulder a comforting pat. "Don't worry. At the first sign of trouble, I'll drag Makoto away. I promise."

"I could lose both of you at one blow." Mel pushed up off the couch. "I'll wear a groove in this floor pacing till you're back safe and sound." He wrung his hands. "I'll be listening to the radio for news bulletins, with my heart in my mouth." He blinked back imaginary tears, and hugged Makoto hard. "You be careful, now. Do you hear me?"

"See you at two-thirty," Makoto said, kissing him, and led Dave quickly out into the night.

Makoto braked his sleek new Accord in front of Mel's house and checked his watch. He grinned at Dave. "Made it," he said. "I always like to keep my promises. Even though he's probably sound asleep."

Dave was dead tired. He pushed open the door on the passenger side, got out, and stretched. Over the shaggy dark ridge of the hills came a glow from the boulevards of the San Fernando Valley to the north. Above, the sky was thick with stars. The air was cool and crisp. It was quiet. He shook Makoto's hand, thanked him, walked to the rickety Valiant—it wouldn't have done to drive it on this expedition—eased his weary self behind the wheel.

Framed in the lighted doorway, Makoto lifted a hand in good-night, stepped inside and closed the door. Dave coaxed the rattly engine of the old car to life, and started down the narrow, parked-up shelves of street, lit by intermittent lamps shining through tree branches. Unlikely as it seemed, all these hairpin curves would finally get him out of the hills. He had to believe that. He wanted very much to be home. Makoto would have driven him, but that would have left the Valiant parked in front of Mel's house. Shocking. Unthinkable.

With Makoto at his side, he'd run into no trouble gaining entry to the Vietnamese clubs on Tracy Davis's list. Old mansions, back rooms of shops, in Monterey Park, at the beach, in the heart of L.A. In five clubs in three hours tonight, he had seen as much green baize as in his whole life, had played more poker hands than in the Army, had rolled more dice, and stared half hypnotized at more roulette wheels than in all the movies of the 1930s. Makoto and he between them had dropped almost a thousand dollars. That had been vital. Baiting a trap, you should look as if you're doing something else. With serious intent. Maybe they'd overdone it. Porcelain-skinned, dark-eyed, mustached little men in tight tuxedos had four times out of five smiled, bowed, shaken their hands, and invited then back as they'd left.

They hadn't overdone it. He knew this a half hour later when he creaked the Valiant up the steep grade of Horseshoe Canyon Trail, and the jittery headlights showed him a black stretch limousine parked at a tilt on the broken road edge opposite his driveway. He geared the Valiant down and climbed toward the parked car slowly, squinting ahead, trying to make out whether or not anyone was inside it. The streetlight was behind him, down where two trails met, and the branches of trees shadowed it, so he got no help from there. The

Valiant's yellow beams glanced off a dazzlingly clean windshield. Heart thudding, he drove past the limousine. If anyone was inside, he couldn't see him.

Thirty yards up the trail, he swung the Valiant in at Wilma Vosper's driveway, backed it up, sat in the middle of the road, motor idling, frowning. Wilma Vosper's raggedy little dog began to bark inside the house. He didn't want to wake her up, and he eased the Valiant down the trail and halted it beside the drop into his bricked yard. He didn't want to look, but he looked. And made out the boxy shape of Cecil's van parked in its usual place, beside the long row of French windows that walled the front building. Sometimes these days when half the crew at the television station was away, he worked very late. Why couldn't tonight have been one of those times?

Dave took a deep breath, and jounced the old car down into the yard. He parked it beside the van, got out, closed the door. It was pitch-dark. Cecil was good at remembering to turn on the ground lights. So somebody else had switched them off. He had expected that someone else—just not so soon. He smiled sourly to himself. It damned well was time he quit. The spring in his step wasn't all he'd lost. The spring in his brain had snapped. A simple phone call could have warned Cecil away, and he hadn't made that call—it simply hadn't crossed his mind. He touched his side. His gun. He'd left it at Mel's. And simply forgotten. Wonderful. Grimly, he crunched over the uneven bricks, rounded the shingled side of the front building, walked into the courtyard where the big oak loomed.

Beyond it the windows of the rear building showed light. Dimly. Through closed curtains. The lantern over the door was dark. He had been surprised there once before. Just a couple of years back. Lurkers had knocked him on the skull while he was pushing his key into the lock. He winced, remembering how his head had ached afterwards. He peered around him, stepped to the slatted bench that circled the thick trunk of the oak. Plants sat there in plastic pots. He picked one up, and lofted it across the courtyard. It struck the door with a thump.

The door burst open, a rectangle of yellow lamplight fell onto the bricks, and a slim little man in black jumped out, and crouched in the light, an Uzi in his delicate hands. His doll face scowled. *Pretty as poison.* He aimed the gun rigidly at Dave. Dave held up his hands. "Don't shoot," he said. "I'm unarmed. I live here." The youngster came out of his crouch, Dave walked toward him. The doll-boy jerked the gun to point Dave at the door. Dave passed him, and walked into the house, the guard behind him, poking his spine with the nose of the Uzi. Dave looked for Cecil, didn't see him. He saw a squat, middle-aged Asian in a dark pin-striped suit, who got up out of one of the leather wing chairs that flanked the fireplace.

Dave asked him, "Where is Cecil Harris?"

"Asleep." The man jerked his head to indicate the loft. The lamplight slid off his greased hair. He came toward Dave with a hand held out. He had a good tailor. A correct inch of shirt cuff showed from under his jacket sleeve. "My name is Don Pham, Mr. Brandstetter." The voice was deep, rough, the accent unmistakeable, but the inflection American.

Dave didn't shake the hand. "What have you done to him?" He started for the raw pine stairs to the loft.

Pham caught his arm. "Don't worry. He's all right. He was very tired. That was easy to see. When we arrived, he got excited." Pham smiled tenderly. "We gave him something to calm him down. He'll be fine in the morning."

"If you've hurt him—" Dave began.

Pham tilted a face pitted with smallpox scars. He said, "What reason would I have to hurt him?" He glanced up at the loft again, and his expression made Dave a little sick. Pham asked, "Have I overlooked something?"

"It's late, and I'm tired myself." Dave moved toward the bar. "If this is going to take long, I need a drink."

Pham followed him, the doll-boy close behind. "Have a drink, by all means," Pham said. He watched Dave find the Glenlivet bottle, a glass, ice cubes. He waited while Dave poured whiskey into the glass, corked the bottle, set it back. "No, thanks," he said with heavy sarcasm, "I don't use it."

Dave only grunted. He started to leave the bar, and Pham reached into a pocket and drew out a paper. Dave knew that paper. His hand went toward his own pocket, then stopped. Someone had bumped into him at the last club. A pickpocket, right? Right. Pham's mouth twitched. He opened the paper and flattened it on the bar.

"San Pedro County," he read aloud, "Office of the Public Defender. Tracy Davis." He blinked at Dave. "How did you come to have this list? What interest does the Public Defender have in Vietnamese gambling clubs?"

Dave shrugged. "I'm just a hired hand. The Public Defender wanted me to visit those places, I visited them." He sketched a smile. "Investigators gather facts. Lawyers put the facts to work. You'll have to ask the lawyers."

"I don't think so," Pham said. "After I was handed this list tonight, I made a phone call to a—friend in the police department. Tracy Davis has been assigned the case of the man accused of the murder of an important member of the Vietnamese community—Le Van Minh. She's trying to shift the blame from her client to one of us. True or false?"

Dave drank from his glass. "Why would she do that?"

"Why would you eat lunch at Hoang Pho?"

"Four wealthy Vietnamese were murdered there, and it's near the Old Fleet Marina, where Le was killed." Dave wanted a cigarette. He'd smoked the pack he'd taken with him. He bent to get a fresh one from under the bar, and the doll-boy made a sound in his throat and stepped close. Dave held up the cigarette pack. The boy glowered. Dave opened the pack, got a cigarette, and lit it. Pham was watching him. Dave said, "I'm not comfortable with coincidences. They always start me looking for the real story."

Pham smiled. "Not just another story? Ms. Davis wants her client freed. Isn't that why she's paying you?"

Dave read his watch. Cotton's DC-10 was thirty-two thousand feet above the black and slumbering Mississippi River by now. He drank from his glass again, and jerked his chin at the bodyguard. "What if I told you that a witness saw two men like your dainty friend here running away from the Old Fleet Marina at the time Le was murdered?"

Pham stared at him without expression. He seemed not to breathe for a minute. He chose his words carefully. "I would say that the witness misunderstood what he saw."

Now it was Dave's turn to stare, his turn to measure his words. "You mean that they were in fact there? But not to kill Le? Is that what I'm to understand?"

"You are to understand," Pham said, "that they did not kill Le Van Minh. On that you have my word."

"I take the word of people I've learned to trust," Dave said. "I don't even know you, Mr. Don."

The smile was crooked and came and went quickly. "My family name is Pham. I have Americanized the order of my names, and dropped the middle one. So, I'm Mr. Pham, but call me Don—I like the name Don, don't you? So American."

"You're in the gambling business," Dave said.

"And the prostitution business." Pham nodded. "And the protection business, and the drug business." He gave a short, sharp laugh. "No, I'm not incriminating myself. I checked this room for electronic listening devices. There aren't any. And your only witness is asleep."

"The crime business, then," Dave said.

Pham inclined his head slightly. "And the crime business is a watchful business, Mr. Brandstetter. I have to know what's going on at all times, in all places. If I get careless, I could end up like Mr. Le."

"Who was not in the crime business?"

Pham laughed. "Quite the reverse. An upright man. An old-fashioned man. A man of conscience."

Dave studied him. "Which made him your enemy, right?"

"Don't be a slave to logic, Mr. Brandstetter." Pham turned and walked away. The bodyguard stayed put, pointing his Uzi at Dave. Pham called, "I and mine had nothing to do with the death of Le Van Minh. Don't waste your time on us. Look into the Le family." He opened the front door. "A wealthy household, Mr. Brandstetter, but a very unhappy one. Old Vietnamese ways clashing with new Western ones." He went out into the dark. The doll-boy, running backwards on silent feet, followed him, and slammed the door.

"Cecil?" Dave ran for the stairs to the loft.

7

Cecil moved angrily, yanking clothes from the hospital room closet. Wire coat hangers flew. His long fingers groped for the ties down the back of the short, starchy garment they'd put on him at four in the morning. By Dave's watch, it was five past eleven, now. The hospital bed coat flapped across the room. Cecil jerked into jockey shorts, a T-shirt. "There were two," he said to Dave. "Two. It took two of them to pin me down."

"All right," Dave said mildly, "there were two. I didn't mean to insult you. I only saw one. The other one must have been out in the car and I missed him."

"Two of the little creeps." Cecil sat in a chair by a tall window, and pulled on socks. "Jumped me in the dark. Otherwise it wouldn't have happened."

"I shouldn't have let you go home," Dave said.

"Hell, how could you know?" Cecil was one leg into his trousers. When Dave had found him lying face down across the wide bed on the loft, those trousers had been

67

dragged down to his knees. Pham and company had stuck him in the butt with a hypodermic. The empty, throw-away syringe lay on the pine chest of drawers. When he'd got Cecil to the UCLA emergency room, they'd told him the injection was morphine. Cecil was staring at him now. "You didn't know, did you?"

"My whole point in going to those clubs," Dave said, "was to get them to surface, whoever they were. No, I didn't know—not that it would happen so soon. All the same, I ought to have called you at work."

Cecil gave a dry laugh. "That way I could have brought a camera crew." He kicked the other leg into the trousers, fastened the waist button, buckled the belt. He picked up his jacket, untangled it from its hanger. He came to Dave, put arms around him, and a kiss on his mouth. He smiled. "Hey, it's not you I'm mad at." He shrugged into the jacket. "It's how I didn't handle it. How they humiliated me."

"They had guns," Dave said. "It wasn't a fair fight."

Cecil grunted, glanced at the room, the unfinished meal on its tray on a swing table over the bed. "Let's get out of here." He yanked open the door and barged, long legged, down the busy corridor. Nurses dodged. Interns with clipboads flattened themselves against walls. A green-clad orderly dropped his mop. Dave half expected Cecil to leap over a lavender-haired lady in a wheelchair. "Why did you bring me here, anyway? Not a thing in the world the matter with me."

"You were limp and cold," Dave said, "and I could hardly hear you breathe." Trying to keep pace with him, Dave remembered the lifetime of cigarettes he'd smoked—right now, his own breathing was doubtful. "Pham is no doctor. He could have overdosed you. I figured I could bring you here, or wait and call the undertaker—right?"

"It's cool." Cecil worked up a smile. Elevator doors opened. Worried-looking families carrying bouquets and new teddy bears crowded out. Cecil and Dave stepped into air damp with the smell of flowers. The elevator doors closed. Cecil pressed a button. "You forget it, I'll forget it."

"Two things I'll be happy to remember," Dave said. "First, Pham hasn't made Cotton Simes as a witness, and second he doesn't connect you to Cotton Simes. At least I don't think so."

"Did his doll-boys kill Le?" Cecil asked.

"He says not." The elevator stopped, the doors opened, they stepped into a lobby teeming with the bandaged and bewildered. "I'll check you out." Dave started for the desk.

Cecil caught his arm, shook his head, urged Dave toward the glass entry doors. "They'll phone when they discover my empty bed. That will be time enough." He pushed out into sunshine, heat, the rustle of wind in trees. "Meanwhile, it will add some excitement to their dull routine." He drew air in gratefully, and skittered like a kid down broad steps. Dave followed slowly, groggy for lack of sleep. Cecil spun around in the lane, arms held out, grinning. "Man, it is so great to be out of there. Nothing I hate worse than hospitals." He gave a shiver. "They keep reminding me of those times when it was you in the bed, and me sitting all night beside you, wondering if you'd live or die." He took Dave's arm and they climbed the gritty steps of gloomy parking levels. In the Valiant, rolling back down to earth, he added, "What happened to your promise to quit?"

"I couldn't get the twenty-two out of my mind." Dave waited for slow traffic to pass, then swung onto a curving lane, over-arched by three branches, and headed off the campus. "The twenty-two makes me think Pham could just possibly be telling the truth. That someone else killed Le."

"Which brings you back to Andy Flanagan?" Cecil said.

"If he owned a twenty-two pistol, the police can't find it. Not on his boat, not underwater." At a stoplight, Dave lit a cigarette. "Which of them there did own a twenty-two pistol? A retired schoolteacher on a pitiful pension living out her sunset years at the Old Fleet, with no place else to go? A young man almost destroyed by bungling doctors and usurious hospitals? With a wife and baby and hardly enough strength to breathe in and out, let alone start over again?" Dave turned the rattly car up Laurel Canyon. "A once famous jazz singer nobody gives a damn for anymore? Even if she can sell the *Starlady*— after that money's gone, then what?"

Cecil stared at him. "You talking about Lindy Willard?"

"What I'm talking about is that I've only interviewed three or four of the boaties."

Cecil nodded. "Which leaves eighty-six to go."

"That's a lot of bunks and lockers to search," Dave said.

"I'd call that a good reason to quit," Cecil said.

Dave swung the Valiant, rattling and complaining, into the broad, clean-swept driveway of Kevin Nakamura's tree-shaded stone and glass service station. He switched off the engine, twisted out the cigarette, stumbled out of the car.

Nakamura, in crisp suntans, came bowlegged and grinning across the tarmac. His eyes very nearly disappeared when he smiled. "What are you? Fed up with the jalopy?" He held out the small cowhide case of the Jaguar's keys.

"I'll take those," Cecil said, and Nakamura tossed

them to him over the top of the Valiant. Cecil loped away
and out of sight behind shiny clean service bays.

"You look beat," Nakamura said. "Everything okay?"

"It will be when I've had twelve hours sleep."

Nakamura laughed and wagged his head. "You'll never
retire. You like playing cops and robbers too much."

"I'm too old for it." Dave touched the Valiant with his
shoe. "Get rid of this. I won't be needing it again."

Nakamura's eyebrows went up. "You sure?"

Dave nodded wearily. "Give whatever you get for it to
your favorite charity."

"That's me," Nakamura said.

And Cecil rolled up in the Jaguar.

When pounding on the door below woke him, the
light in the sky above the open roof window was ruddy.
The air had cooled. He squinted at the bedside clock. Its
red numerals said it was five forty-five. He groaned,
pushed himself into a sitting position, swung numb legs
over the bed side. Blinking, blowing out air, he looked
around for the blue corduroy robe. There it was, draped
over the two-by-four railing of the loft. He lit a cigarette,
wavered to his feet, fumbled into the robe. Muttering
because he hadn't the energy to shout, he tottered down
the stairs. Making for the door, broad pine planks cool
under his bare feet, he combed back his hair with his
fingers, rubbed a hand down over his face. He said
hoarsely, "Who is it?"

"Open up, Sherlock. I want to talk to you." It was Ken
Barker, a captain in the homicide division of the LAPD.
Dave had known him for twenty years, as he'd come up
through the ranks from plain detective. They had begun
on bad terms. But they'd butted heads so often, enmity
had turned to grudging respect and finally to what they
both knew was friendship, though a stranger watching

them together might not guess it. Dave worked two locks and pulled open the door. Barker, heavy now, almost as thick through the middle as across his massive shoulders, glowered at him. He had steel gray eyes that never relented. The broken nose between them gave him the toughest look on the force. Dave stepped back to let him pass, and closed the door again.

"You woke me up," Dave said.

"I didn't know you ever slept," Barker said. "How do you find the time, making all the trouble you do?"

Dave smiled thinly, held up his hands. "Not guilty." He turned and went away toward the bar. "Sit down. I'll fix you a drink."

Barker dropped his bulk into one of the leather wing chairs. His voice rumbled, echoing off the high pitched roof and bare rafters. "You checked Harris into UCLA hospital in the wee small hours. OD'd on morphine. He an addict?"

Dave was still so tired, he seemed to be watching himself in a slow-motion film as he got glasses, Glenlivet for himself, Jack Daniels for Barker, filled the glasses with ice cubes, uncapped the bottles, poured the drinks, recapped the bottles. He carried them to the hearth, handed Barker the sourmash, sat down on the raised brick surround of the fireplace, tasted his drink. "Why ask me? You've already been to see him at Channel Three."

Barker grunted. "It figured he'd phone and warn you."

"Wrong. Phones here are unplugged." Dave threw him a half smile. "No—I just know how you work."

Barker's mouth twitched. He lifted his glass to Dave, and drank from it. "Ah. That hits the spot." Dave thought it should. Barker kept damned bad liquor in his office—the only place he'd ever offered Dave a drink. "Harris denied it. Said it was an accident."

"I've never known him to lie. What can I say?"

"You keep morphine around here?" Barker asked. He glanced towards the bathroom at the foot of the stairs. He glanced at the sleeping loft. "You want to show me? You want to show me the prescription?"

"There's no prescription," Dave said. "No morphine."

"What happened?" Barker said.

"I'm working a case for a public defender in San Pedro County." Dave outlined the story—the trouble at the Old Fleet, Le Van Minh's murder, Andy Flanagan's arrest. "I'm trying to turn up another suspect. In doing so, I bumped a hornet's nest. The head hornet came here last night to warn me off. I wasn't home, yet, and Cecil got stung."

"Wrong man in the wrong place at the wrong time?"

"As he told you—an accident." Dave set his glass on the bricks. He got up to get cigarettes and lighter from the bar. It seemed a long time since he'd opened the new pack there, with the doll-boy watching it as if it were a grenade. It was only fifteen hours ago. He lit a cigarette, put pack and lighter in a pocket of the robe, went back to Barker. "It might have been a lot worse." He sat on the hearth again, and drank again. "They could have killed him."

"You get nice visitors," Barker said.

"It's hard to find words," Dave said.

"You didn't report it to us. You going to report it to the police department down in San Pedro County?"

"I'll tell Tracy Davis when I see her. She'll tell the police." He gave Barker a blank, wide-eyed look. "I mean, won't she? It's her duty, isn't it?"

"This happened in my territory," Barker said heavily. "And it happened to a friend of a friend of mine. A flake, but a friend, and I don't like that." He drank deeply of his Jack Daniels. He thumped the bottom of the thick glass on the chair arm and the ice cubes rattled. "And I'm not going to let it happen again." He fixed Dave with that cold steel stare of his. "If San Pedro won't protect you, I will."

"This crowd is through with me." The fire screen was accordioned back. Dave flicked ashes into the grate. "They won't come again." He gave Barker a sidewise glance. Barker didn't look persuaded. "Honest. I don't think so."

Barker snorted. "What do they think?"

"That I now know I was wrong about them, and that I'm going to leave them alone from here on out."

Barker heaved his bulk up out of the chair. He looked down at Dave. Skeptically. "And will you?" He wheeled like a truck and headed for the door. "Not if I know you. If there's an excuse to go after them, you'll go after them, regardless of the risk." He pulled the door open. Dusk had come and filled the courtyard with shadow. He turned back. "Who are they, Dave? I need to know."

"A Vietnamese named Don Pham, who runs gambling clubs in San Pedro County." Dave rose and limped on leaden legs to tell Barker the other activities Pham had admitted to. Or bragged of. "He had two nasty little thugs with him. They dress in black jeans, black turtleneck jerseys, sometimes cover their faces with black handkerchiefs. Favorite weapon, the Uzi. There may be only two"—he shrugged bleakly—"there could be twenty."

"With the morals of weasels," Barker said. "I know the type. They're hell to catch. They've got the law-abiding Vietnamese here terrified. Nobody dares tell on them." He sighed. "And the Vietnamese are only part of the picture. There are Samoans, Tongans, Filipinos, Koreans, Laotians, Cambodians." He gave his head a grim shake. "It's a restless world today, and we seem to get whatever it shakes out. They come here without education, without any language but their own—crime is what keeps them eating." He took a step or two away across the bricks. He looked up at the sky, where there was still some dying daylight. "I'm just as glad I'm retiring. This mess needs a new kind of cop."

"That will be nice," Dave said. "The old kind was a pain in the ass."

"Hah!" Barker said. "Look who's calling who a pain in the ass." He peered at Dave through the twilight. "You don't want me to post a man up here? To keep an eye out?"

"If you've forgotten," Dave said, "I haven't. People who try to guard me get shot. Joey Samuels still isn't back at work—is he?"

"He will be," Barker said. "Stop feeling guilty. It wasn't your fault. He was doing a job. It happens to police officers. They know it. They're fatalists. It tends to limit their friendships. Only other cops understand."

Barker was lonely and wanted to talk. Dave said, "I can dress. We can have dinner together. Max Romano's." But before he could finish speaking, he yawned.

"Go back to bed," Barker said, and lumbered off.

After that, Dave slept the clock around. Almost. No way could he not be aware of Cecil's coming home from work at midnight. Very few nights in recent years had he tried to sleep before that happened. Cecil moved quietly, but Dave took in that he was down below, heard him locking up, water running in the pipes as he showered, the click of switches as he turned off lamps, his footfalls on the stairs. Familiar floorboards creaked as he moved on the loft, shedding his clothes. The bed jarred gently as he slid under sheet and blanket. Dave felt the warmth of his long, lean body, and smiled to himself. Now he could really sleep.

And sleep he did.

"Don't you feel a little ghoulish?" Cecil said. He brought plates to the table in the cook shack. It was going to be another hot day. The door stood open. It wasn't yet seven o'clock, and the still air was oppressive.

Horn-rimmed reading glasses on his nose, Dave was checking the obituary columns. The name "Le" was where he expected it. "Maybe." He took off the glasses, frowning. "I'm trying to remember. There was another Le listed here not long ago."

"Sounds like it might be a common name," Cecil said.

"True, but the mortuary was the same. The church was the same." Dave folded the paper, laid it aside.

Cecil set a plate in front of him. Fried cornmeal mush. Thick rounds of Canadian bacon. Eggs sunny-side up. Cecil brought a stoneware jug of Vermont maple syrup to the table, pulled out a chair beside Dave's and sat down. He wore a long yellow and black tanktop stenciled LAKERS, ragged white cutoffs, white golfer's cap pulled low over his eyes.

"This looks delicious," Dave told him. "So do you. And smiling all over, too. What's up?"

"Jimmy Caesar and Dot Yamada get back from vacation today." Cecil cut pats of butter onto his golden squares of hash. He set the butter plate down. "'Free at last, I'm free at last.'" He poured syrup over the mush, cut a bite from the bacon, a bite from the mush, speared both with his fork, filled his mouth, hummed, and closed his eyes. When he'd chewed and swallowed and gulped down some coffee, he said, "Today, we build those bookshelves."

Dave hated to cloud all that joy, but he gave his head a

shake. "I'm sorry." He tapped the folded paper with a finger. "I've got a funeral to attend."

"You mean Le's?" Cecil squinted. "Why?"

"The usual reason."

"He was rich and powerful." Cecil broke a yolk on one of his eggs, muddled a chunk of the crisp fried mush in it, filled his mouth again. "People will be there who don't mean anything. Most of them."

"I want a look at the family." Dave tucked into his breakfast. It tasted as good as it looked, and he was very hungry. When it was time to breathe again, he said, "And I want to see if Don Pham shows up."

"Stick a needle in his butt for me," Cecil said. "What connection would there be?"

"He seems to know the Le's." Dave drank coffee. "And he's in the drug business."

"Le was an importer," Cecil said. "Electronics. From the Orient." He tilted his head. "You saying suppliers were sending Pham opium inside the VCRs?"

"Suppose Le had found out about it? Pham's doll-boys went to the Old Fleet for a reason—and it wasn't to watch late TV with Norma Potter. I have only Pham's word they didn't kill Le, and he carefully did not say they didn't go there to kill him, and my hunch is that if they didn't do it, it was only because somebody else got to him first."

"You have a mind like a whip." Cecil mopped up the egg yolk and syrup on his plate with a last chunk of mush. He grumbled, "You are in this to the end, aren't you? That retirement jive was jive and only jive, right? And I am going to be here alone today, sawing up boards, banging my thumb with a hammer while you—"

"The funeral's this morning." Dave looked at his watch, gulped coffee, wiped his mouth with a napkin.

"I'll be back by noon. We can take turns banging our thumbs."

"You say." Cecil scraped his chair back, stood and gathered the plates. Gloomily. "When you get out there, you'll find a dozen reasons not to come home."

Dave stood, put a kiss on his mouth. "Knowing you're here, nothing less than wild horses could keep me away."

Cecil grunted, walked off. "Not too many of them around the harbor." He set the dishes in the sink. "But knowing you, you'll find them." He turned on the hot water tap.

Dave paused at the door. "Why not come with me?"

Cecil shook his head. "One ghoul per family is enough."

8

The Vietnamese Methodist church was white stucco, a try at Spanish mission style that had got the proportions wrong. There was too much height to it, not enough spread. Its location was against it too, on a corner in a dying neighborhood of dejected brick storefronts and thick, spiky-trunked old date palms on trash-strewn parking strips. A sea wind that smelled of spilled oil waved the half-dead palm fronds above rows of sleek, showy automobiles at the curbs, FUNERAL on a white card behind each windshield.

The pews were filled when Dave arrived, and he stood at the back of the sanctuary through the service—the ritual and prayers, the solemn words from a local white politician in English, the eulogies by the minister, by a fortyish man Dave guessed to be Le's son, and by two older men, friends or business associates, or maybe both, in Vietnamese.

The pallbearers—the bald assemblyman towering over the five Vietnamese, the only thing relating them their dark business suits—brought the flower-covered coffin out the varnish-peeling front doors of the church and down cracked cement stairs to the hearse. The family followed. News cameras whirred and clicked.

A tiny, very old, imperious-looking dowager walked on the arm of a smartly dressed woman Dave took to be Le's widow. The fortyish son and his wife had a teen-aged son and daughter with them. There followed a pretty Vietnamese woman in her twenties accompanied by a man of the same age, conspicuously American, blond, blue-eyed, good looking. Each had a small child by the hand. The smooth faces of the children were Oriental but their hair was pale gold. Something about their father stirred a memory in Dave. He'd seen him before. Not lately. A few years ago. Where?

Trailing them came a willowy Vietnamese girl of maybe eighteen. While everyone else was stoical, dry-eyed, she was weeping into a handkerchief. Part of the family? He didn't think so, yet she did get into one of the glossy gray limousines the funeral directors had lined up to carry the blood kin and kin by marriage of Le Van Minh to the cemetery. Dave stayed behind to study the rest of the mourners. Don Pham was not among them. Maybe only because of the cameras.

The procession reached the gravesite by winding through a gloomy old burial ground of untrimmed trees and shrubs and tilted, mossy headstones. Beyond this, raw acreage had been recently opened. This new part scarcely had a lawn yet, let alone a tree. The sun beat down on plaques in the tender new grass, the plaques all spotless, the dates of death recent, the names all Vietnamese.

The family sat on gray steel folding chairs under a canvas pavilion on a frame of chrome-plated tubing. The girl stood behind the two rows of chairs. Dave watched from a distance as the minister read words at the head of the grave, but it wasn't the minister he watched. Nor, more than casually, the family. It was the girl. She stood rigid, fists clenched, appeared to force herself to look at the casket with its burden of flowers, to make an effort to listen, remember, respect—then she would turn sharply and look away, biting her lips. Why? What made her grief seem more painful than that of all the other mourners? Why did she look as if she wanted to break and run? The teen-aged boy kept watching her too, worried. Dave suspected he was in love with her.

The ancient words of comfort from the prayerbook neared their end. The middle-aged son got off his chair, stooped for a handful of earth, scattered it into the grave. In benediction, the high voice of the squat, bespectacled minister drifted to Dave on the oven-hot air, and he turned away and trudged across the fragile grass, back to the Jaguar at the end of the long line of parked cars that had made up Le Van Minh's cortege. He switched on the engine, waited till the vents in the burled instrument panel blew cold air at him, shut the car door, lit a cigarette, and read his watch. Half past eleven. Cecil was going to be surprised. Dave smiled and swung the softly rumbling car out onto the new blacktop of the lane. He was surprised, himself.

A car swung past him, a dented ten-year-old Japanese hatchback. Scuffed leather carryalls lay tangled in shoulder straps in the back. The kind that photographers stowed cameras in, lenses, light meters, film. A wrinkled bumper sticker said READ THE HARBOR BULLETIN. The car's exhaust pipe pumped brown smoke onto the blacktop. Dave followed it closely. At the folded-back wrought-iron gates of the old cemetery, the driver half stopped to let street traffic pass. Dave pulled up beside him, and tapped the Jaguar's horn. The hatchback driver was a fat kid with a beard. He winced at Dave. Dave rolled down the Jaguar's window.

"Let me buy you a cup of coffee," he called.

The bearded one cocked a doubtful eyebrow, read a wristwatch. "I have to get back to the paper."

"I work for the Public Defender," Dave called. "I need your help. It won't take long."

The fat kid shrugged unhappily, pointed up the block. "Follow me."

The place was a shack on a corner, with an open-air counter, three stools, a strong smell of hot grease. Coffee came in Styrofoam cups. The kid, whose name was Marlon Thornberg, ate doughnuts with his coffee. Dave said:

"Do you write or just take pictures?"

"I do it all," Thornberg said, spraying crumbs. "We all do it all. It's a small paper for a daily."

"Do you take turns on every story?" Dave took out a cigarette. "Or do the Le's belong to you?"

"Don't smoke around me," Thornberg said. "I have asthma." He watched Dave put the cigarette back into the pack. "The Le's belong to me." He licked chocolate frosting off his fat fingers. "Why?"

"What have you learned?"

"Le Van Minh, his mother, wife, two sons, daughter, daughter-in-law, and two little grandchildren came here when the Americans decamped in 1975. Le was a successful businessman there, but he had to leave everything behind to the Communists, okay?" Thornberg picked up a second doughnut and eyed it hungrily. "They were given permanent residence status here."

"Two sons?" Dave said. "I only saw one today. Am I right? The one who delivered the eulogy, the one who picked up the handful of dust?"

Thornberg washed chewed doughnut down with coffee. He nodded. "That was Le Tran Hai. The oldest son. His brother died a few weeks ago." He took another big bite of doughnut. "He was only thirty."

"I thought I'd seen the obituary. How did he die?"

Chewing, Thornberg pointed at his stuffed mouth. He finally swallowed, slurped more coffee. "Died in his sleep. It happens to young Vietnamese males. Nobody knows why."

"What did he do for a living?"

"Worked for his old man. So does Hai. The younger son—his name was Ba. You know how they get those names?" He poked the remainder of the doughnut into his mouth. Dave looked away at the scruffy street. The hearse passed, the limousines, some of the cars that had made up the funeral procession. "The first born is always Hai, the second Ba—nicknames, really." He licked his fingers. "And it doesn't matter if it's a boy or a girl."

"Died in his sleep. It must have been a shock. Did Mr. Le take it badly?"

"You couldn't tell it from how he acted," Thornberg said. "But his daughter told me it broke the old man's heart. He loved Ba the most of all his children. Ba was no good as a worker. He was a dreamer, a poet. The old man would have let him sit in his room and write. But to be fair to Hai, he insisted Ba do his share at the warehouse."

"There's only one daughter, the young one I saw with the two little kids and the young Anglo?"

"Her name's Quynh." He pronounced it "Queen," and he spelled it for Dave. "Her husband's named Matt Fergusson. He pretty much runs those restaurants for Madame Le."

"Who's the other beautiful girl?" Dave said.

"Family friend. Visiting. Lives in Paris with her father. Name's Thao." He leered. "Outstanding, right?"

"She's very attractive," Dave said, "and very cut up. Le's widow owns restaurants?"

"Vietnamese food." Thornberg made a face. "I don't know how people can eat that garbage." He leaned in at the service window. "Got any more of those chocolate doughnuts?"

"Does she own Hoang Pho?" Dave said.

A brown hand came out the service window. It held two more chocolate doughnuts in a paper napkin. A voice spoke words Dave couldn't make out. Thornberg struggled to dig money from the pocket of a sausage-tight pair of jeans.

"I've got it." Dave laid two dollars in the hand.

"Thanks," Thornberg said. "What name did you say?"

"Hoang Pho," Dave said, "the Vietnamese restaurant down near the Old Fleet Marina. Where those business-men were machine-gunned not long ago."

"Jesus, what a story that was," Thornberg said. "Talk about doors slammed in your face. Nobody, but nobody, was going to say word one about that."

"You could ask Don Pham," Dave said.

Thornberg, about to bite one of the new doughnuts, did not bite. He raised his eyebrows. "The gambling boss?"

"Him." Dave nodded. "The Hoang Pho?" he prompted.

"No, that belongs to Hoang Duc Nghi. It's not one of Madam Le's. Hers are at Newport Harbor and near the university, places like that. Upscale." Thornberg bit his doughnut, and said with his mouth full, "Not really, but almost." He frowned while he chewed, drank coffee, set down the empty cup. "Public Defender's office? Who's being defended?" He blinked. "You mean Andy Flanagan, the one who shot Le?"

"The one they jailed for shooting Le," Dave said. "The PD doesn't think he did it. And I'm beginning to agree."

Thornberg grunted, ran his tongue around his teeth, thought for a minute. "You think it was Don Pham?"

"Gambling isn't his only interest. And he has a team of little thugs who dress in black and carry Uzis. Rumor has it they were at the Old Fleet the night Le was killed."

"Which could connect Le's murder with the ones at the Hoang Pho?" Thornberg said. "Yeah. I see where you're coming from. Heavy."

"I didn't read your story about the Hoang Pho killings," Dave said. "The one in the L.A. *Times* said an employee of the restaurant described the killers. It didn't give that employee's name. Did your story give the name?"

"The police didn't release it," Thornberg said.

"And you didn't dig him up yourself?" Dave said.

Thornberg laughed glumly. "Hoang couldn't remember any names. He didn't have any records. Sorry." For the first time Thornberg seemed really to look at Dave. "I think I know you, don't I? From somewhere?"

"I don't think so." Hastily Dave left his stool. "I appreciate your help."

"Hey." Thornberg's fat-boy face in its frame of bushy black beard lit up. He snapped his fingers and pointed. "*Newsweek*. They did a profile on you last year, right? Sure." He got his bulk off the creaky stool, eager, excited. "I have to write about this. How come you're on this case? It can't be insurance—Flanagan hasn't got a dime."

"Off the record," Dave said, "the Public Defender is his half-sister, okay? She cares. She hired me."

"The best in the business, yeah. Oh, boy." He started toward his car. "Let me get my camera."

"Not today," Dave said. "There's no story, yet."

"You're the story," Thornberg said. "You're famous."

"I need to keep a low profile on this," Dave said. "You help me with that, and I promise, when it's over, I'll give you an exclusive interview."

"Oh, sure you will." Thornberg slouched away.

Dave called after him. "Meantime, I wouldn't write about Don Pham, either, if I were you. Not if you want to go on eating the health foods you so enjoy."

"I know, I know." Thornberg got into his car, slammed the door, started the clattering engine. "Thanks for the doughnuts," he said sulkily, and drove off in a cloud of oily smoke.

The docks weren't what they had been. Other harbors got most of the shipping now. Nothing much was doing here. Nobody was around. Freighters sat rusting in sluggish water that mirrored them, turning to slate gray their bands of red and yellow paint. They flew flags of Greece, Panama, Japan, Hong Kong, Singapore, and flags he couldn't name. It seemed as if Pier Nine had only one operative warehouse—the rest looked boarded up. Double gates that would have let him drive the Jaguar out on the wharf were locked. A sign was strung to the mesh. Hand-lettered on a shirt cardboard with a blue magic marker pen, it explained about the funeral, and that business would be suspended for the day out of respect for the dead.

Well, he didn't need to drive out there. He could walk. He went down a splintery set of stairs beside the truck ramp. What drew him was a car parked by the warehouse doors—a new car, four-door, paint glossy, windows glittering in the glare of the sun. There was a second car, farther on, but that one was old and battered, probably the wheels of the security guard. Assignments like this paid minimum wage. Whoever took them couldn't afford fancy transportation. A security guard would belong here. But who else would—on the day of Le Van Minh's burial?

He passed through the crisscross shadow of the crane he'd seen from the Old Fleet, hoisting a freight container off a ship. He walked on between stacks of enormous empty crates that smelled of pine sap in the heat. He bent and peered inside the handsome car. It smelled of newness. On the floor behind the front seats lay a new baseball glove. That was all there was to look at. Dave stepped back and studied the car, frowning. Had it rolled along to the cemetery in the funeral procession? No. Its wine-red color he'd have noticed. Now he memorized the license number.

He winced up at the white face of the warehouse. LE ELECTRONIC IMPORTS, LTD. Weather was hard on signs by the ocean. The black lettering was beginning to scale. He moved to the enormous doors. Bolted and locked several times over. A door of human dimensions was set into one of the giant panels, but when he tried it, quietly, it wouldn't budge. It was a big warehouse. He hiked along to the far corner. The side wall had windows in it, but high, and of opaque wired glass. None was open for him to look in through or climb in through, if he found a way to get up to it. He heard the engine of a power boat, started toward the sound, and a voice said:

"Hold it right there." A skinny old man was pointing a revolver at him. The man wore suntans with blue oval patches on the sleeves and on one shirt pocket. The patches were stitched in gold DRYCOTT SECURITY SERV-ICES. "What's your business here? Don't you know you're trespassing?"

"I didn't know that," Dave said.

Wind off the water stirred the old man's thin white hair. His faded eyes looked past Dave. Anxiously. Worrying about the power boat. He motioned with the gun barrel. "Well, you are, and I'm going to have to ask you to leave."

"I'm an investigator for the Public Defender's Office." Dave reached for the folder that held his license. The old man jerked the gun and made a sound like "Hup. Keep your hands where I can see 'em. You got business here, come when it's open." He kept glancing nervously toward the boat. "Closed today. Funeral."

"The funeral's over," Dave said. "I was there." He turned now to see what the old man was seeing. It was a sleek white cabin cruiser, a forty-footer. A muscular young Asian in the prow, naked to the waist, wore a red neckerchief. He saw Dave and the security guard, turned, shouted something astern. And the boat veered off, started to make a circle in the harbor, and the circle took it out of sight, behind a freighter. Dave looked at the old man. He appeared relieved. He almost forgot to scowl at Dave.

"On your way, now. Come back tomorrow."

Dave trudged back up the thick, tarred planks of the pier, climbed the zigzag steps, got into the Jaguar, and drove away. He didn't look back. He was sure he was being watched, by the guard, and by the red neckerchief on the boat. But he didn't drive far. He swung off into a side street, made a right turn, and another right turn onto another side street, and left the Jaguar there. He walked in the shadow of shop awnings back to where he could see the wharf. He pushed open a shop door and found himself in a real estate office. A desk that faced the window had a blowsy blonde woman seated at it. She

wore a lot of paint and junk jewelry. She blinked warily
at him. He showed her his license.

"May I sit there for a few minutes?"

"Well"—she looked from him to the license and back
again, flustered—"I really don't think I—"

While he looked out the window, watching the power
cruiser approach the wharf, he got out his wallet, took a
fifty-dollar bill from it, laid it on the desk. He gave her
his warmest smile. "That's for your trouble," he said.

She stood up, looked around for advice, but since the
place was empty, didn't get any. She made a quick grab at
the bill, flinched a smile at Dave, and backed away.
Scared but intrigued. "Yes—all right," she said.

"Just go on with your work." Dave sat down. It was a
secretarial chair, with springs and swivels. It had been
sat in by one person for too long. It wasn't ready for a
new backside. It nearly threw him. He grabbed the desk
edge and righted himself. "I won't be here long."

Red neckerchief tossed a line up to the dock. The
security guard wrapped it around a cleat.

The real estate woman whispered, "Is it a murder
case?"

"That's right," Dave said.

"How exciting." Her voice trembled and squeaked.

A thick-set man wearing sunglasses climbed a ladder
to the wharf from the launch. He spoke to the security
guard, and then the two of them walked to the doors of
the Le warehouse. The old man in suntans, with his gun
back in its holster on his skinny hip, turned keys in
locks in the small door, and the two of them disappeared
inside. The door closed. Was the thick-set man Don
Pham?

Dave turned cautiously in the risky chair. "You don't
have a pair of binoculars here anywhere, do you?"

The blonde woman looked around again. She was

pale. Her painty rosebud mouth trembled. "I—I don't think so. No." She wrung her hands, showed little white teeth, and tried for a joke. "We don't do bird-watching, as a rule."

"I was thinking"—Dave smiled—"of sailor-watching."

"What? Oh." She tittered, not meaning it.

"You've got a great desk for it," Dave said.

"I'm married," she said primly.

Dave gave his head a rueful shake. "I should have known." He turned back to the window with a sigh. "The attractive ones always are."

"And I have my career," she said. "I haven't time for love affairs. Even if I wanted them. Sailors? Please!"

The door of the warehouse opened. The security guard came out first, took a step away from the door, and looked carefully up and down the wharf. He turned his head and spoke. And the thick-set man came out again. He carried attaché cases, one in each hand. He still wore the dark glasses. Dave still couldn't tell if he was Don Pham. He moved off toward the waiting cruiser gleaming in the sun.

A third man came out of the warehouse. He wore a jogging outfit. A baseball cap was pushed back on his hair. His hair was gold. The thick-set man dropped the attaché cases to Red Neckerchief, climbed down the ladder, stepped onto the deck. The jogger bent and unlashed the painter from its cleat for Red Neckerchief to gather up and coil. The thick-set man carried the cases aft. The cruiser's engine started. The jogger waved an arm, and the cruiser curved away, churning up a big wake in the still gray water. The man in the jogging suit spoke to the security guard, got into the wine-red car, began to turn it around on the dock.

Dave stood up. "Where can I get out of sight?"

She waved at the back of the shop. He went that way.

An inner office had a computer on its desk. He passed a water cooler, a washroom door. He turned the lock on a back door, stepped into an alley, and headed for the Jaguar.

It was twilight. The room was in shadow. He tripped over lumber on the floor. He didn't fall. He only stubbed a toe. He stood wincing for a minute, to let his eyes get accustomed to the dimness, then he picked his way among boards, scraps of board, sawhorses, circular saw, planer, sander, and their snaking electric cords, to a lamp on a table at the end of the couch. He had got the uprights for the bookshelves spiked into place, ten feet tall, right up to the rafters, and three feet apart. He'd spaced one-by-two cleats up them, to hold the shelves that would come later. An envelope was nailed to one of the uprights. Dave jerked it down, tore it open, unfolded the page inside.

> *Next time, maybe you'll listen to me. But don't worry. Any demand for ransom Don Pham sends, under seventy-eight cents, which is all I have in my pockets, I will pay. Be patient, though. Counting all that money will be slow going because, while I did not bash my thumb today, I did pick up splinters. If you are not a prisoner, or up to your ankles in cement at the bottom of the Old Fleet Marina, maybe you can meet me for dinner at Max's. I have bribed Dan Rather to fill in for me between 8:00 and 9:00 at work, so I'll hope to see you.*
> *—C.H. (Pure Cane Sugar)*

Grinning, Dave headed for the shower.

9

The sun blazed down on a black and red freighter that lay alongside the dock. The crew of the freighter, underfed, shock-headed Asians in skivvy shirts and stained white jeans, winched crates up out of open hatches. Chains rattled, gears clashed, engines strained and snarled. Jabbering, the men unhooked the lines from the winches, and waited, squinting upwards at the unforgiving sky, hands shielding their eyes—waited for the long steel cables of the high crane on the dock to lower hammocks of rope mesh to cradle the crates, hoist them, swing them dockside, where the broad front of the Le warehouse glared white, the shadows of gulls flickering across it.

On the dock, sturdy Anglos, blacks, Latinos in battered hardhats stripped the rope mesh off the crates. Yellow forklifts bucked forward to pick up the crates. The crane swept the empty nets skyward. The warehouse doors stood open today. The forklifts jerkily backed and filled, and whined between those doors, carrying the crates into vast darkness. Flanking the doorway, men in suits watched the forklifts pass and made checkmarks on clipboards. One of these men was Le Tran Hai, the older Le son. Dave didn't know the other man, middle-aged, gray-faced, thick glasses. An accountant?

Stepping around crates, glancing upward to keep out of range of the crane and its swinging cables, Dave moved toward the Vietnamese. The noise level was high—shouts, laughter, the crane's engine, the whine of the forklifts, the thud of the heavy crates on the planks of the wharf, the whoops of tugs in the harbor. Dave figured he'd better get Hai's attention before he tried speaking to him. He tapped his shoulder. Hai shrugged annoyance, made a face, scowled at the manifest on his clipboard. He ran a ballpoint pen along the computer-printed cargo list, down the list, up again, finally found the item he wanted, slashed a check beside it, turned sharply to Dave.

"What is it?" he snapped. "Who are you?"

Dave showed him his license. "Can we talk inside?"

Another forklift bumped past. Hai studied the list on the clipboard again, marked off another item. "You're kidding. I'm busy. Can't you see that?"

"I'll wait," Dave said.

"What's it about?" Hai said.

"Your father's murder," Dave said, and stepped away.

Hai caught his arm. "You can't wait out here. It's dangerous. Go inside. The office. Upstairs at the back. I'll come as soon as I can."

It was dangerous inside, too. He was nearly flattened by a forklift. They moved fast. Dave heard or felt the thing at his back not quite in time to jump aside. A corner of a moving crate slammed into him, sent him reeling against crates already stacked. The driver yelped surprise, stopped the forklift, jumped off it, came to him, whitefaced under his red hardhat. An identity badge hung off a chain around his neck. *Herman Steinkrohn.* He was big, young, blond, scared. "Jesus. I'm sorry. Are you okay?"

Dave rubbed his shoulder. His heart thudded. His knees felt weak. He tried to smile. "It's nothing."

"I didn't see you." Steinkrohn bent and picked up the thick manila envelope Dave had dropped. He handed it back to him. "Sure you're not hurt? You want a doctor?"

"Thanks. I don't want to get you into trouble. It was entirely my fault." Dave said. "I was where I didn't belong. Mr. Le told me to wait in the office."

The kid pointed upwards. The curved roof of the warehouse high above was supported by a cross stitching of lacy steel beams and struts. A narrow slat-floored metal walkway ran along the side maybe eighteen feet above this floor. "Why don't you climb the stairs over there"—he pointed with a work-gloved finger—"and go along the catwalk. You won't get bumped into there." Steinkrohn climbed onto the seat of the forklift, shifted gears. "Office is way at the back. Listen, thanks. If I can ever do anything for you, let me know." He drove on up the long narrow aisle.

Dave climbed steel stairs, hiked along the clacking frets of the steel catwalk to boxy steel and glass offices at the rear. Hard fluorescent light shone down on desks, file cabinets, computers. Printers whined and beeped and poured out long tongues of lined paper. Telephones rang. Typewriters rattled. Desktop calculators clicked and buzzed. Six or eight young Vietnamese manned the office. All very neat in their dress, all strictly tending to business. A young woman gathering up computer print-outs from the pale vinyl tile floor, saw him, smiled, called out:

"May I help you?"

She sat him down in a quiet office and brought him a paper cup of coffee. The office was simply outfitted. The desk and chairs were metal with fake leather cushions. It was a place to work in, not to get comfortable in. Only one touch contrasted it to the busy offices surrounding it. A vase of deftly arranged flowers on the desk. He hadn't finished the coffee when Hai came in, carrying a can of soda, went and sat back of his desk, looked at Dave and said:

"I can only give you a few minutes. You picked a very busy day. Do I understand that you are looking into the death of my father in defense of the man who killed him?"

"Of the man the police think killed him," Dave said.

Hai's brows rose. "And you do not think so?" He had almost no Vietnamese accent. The foreignness of his speech showed up in the stilted way he put his sentences together. "I saw you at my father's funeral, did I not? Standing at the back of the church?"

"That's right."

"Why? Do you think it was some member of the household who killed him? Me? My sister? My mother? We were all at home. I have watched my share of detective shows on television. Surely you do not think as they think"—he gave a thin, disbelieving smile—"or act as they act. That is make-believe. The murder of my father was reality."

"I try not to confuse the two," Dave said. "I've been in the business of investigating unexplained sudden deaths all my life. One thing comes first. Talk to everybody you can find who knew the man or woman who was killed. And that, of course"—he used a tight little smile of his own—"includes his family."

After eyeing Dave for a moment, Hai gave a quick nod.

Dave said, "Actually, I'm more interested in a man called Don Pham, right now. Do you know him?"

Hai's look was guarded. He said, "No," carefully.

"He operates gambling establishments, prostitution rings," Dave said, "and he deals in illegal drugs."

"I wouldn't know such a person," Hai said.

"He seems to know a lot about you and the rest of the Le family. How come?"

"I can't say." Hai read his watch, drank some soda. "My father's business success made him prominent in the community. This sometimes meant we were written about in the newspapers and spoken about on television. So the Le family and its doings were scarcely as private as he would have liked them to be."

"Your father never mentioned Don Pham?" Dave said.

Hai's laugh was scornful. "Why would he? My father always demanded of us that we live up to the highest standards, and he himself would never set a poor example to his children. Associating with a criminal?" He pushed back his chair, got to his feet. "It is out of the question."

Dave stood up too. "What about Rafe Carpenter?"

Hai had started to come around the desk. He stopped in mid-stride and squinted at Dave. "What do you mean?"

"Would you call him a friend—or only an employee?"

"Rafe has worked here a very long time," Hai said. "Almost from the start. My father placed a great deal of trust in him. He is a hard worker. He helped to build this business." Hai blinked. "Have you discovered something to his discredit?"

"Do you pay him bonuses?" Dave said. "In cash?"

Puzzled, Hai said, "At Christmas? Yes. We give all our employees Christmas bonuses." He frowned. "In cash? That would be wrong, Mr. Brandstetter. As guests in your country, my father taught us to be scrupulous in observing all laws. And seeing to it that our employees do the same. Cash payments might go unreported"— again he used that token smile of his—"to the IRS. No, the bonuses are paid by check, with all deductions taken out, according to the rules."

"Somebody's been paying him cash bonuses," Dave said. "Big cash bonuses. And not just at Christmas." He laid the brown envelope on Hai's desk, pried up the fasteners, opened the flap, pulled out computer print-outs. "Look at these, please." He spread them on the desk. Frowning, Hai sat in his chair again, and bent over the green-meshed documents. Mel Fleischer, after yelps and moans of protest, had got these for Dave this morning. Dave had picked them up at his office. Now, Hai traced the figures on the sheets with a ballpoint pen, as he'd done with the shipping manifests out on the dock. He looked up at Dave. "What do these mean?"

"They mean that for the past thirteen or fourteen months, Rafe Carpenter has been receiving hefty pay-ments from somebody for something. He's bought a three-hundred-thousand-dollar house with an ocean view."

Hai nodded. "He invited me to dinner there."

"And it didn't seem odd to you that a warehouseman earning union scale could afford to live like that?"

Hai flushed. "A guest does not question such things."

"That's an eighteen-thousand-dollar car he's driving these days," Dave said. "His wife has a brand-new station wagon. He's sending his kid to a fancy private school. Where's the money coming from, Mr. Le?"

"Not from here." Hai pushed the papers away from him.

"Did he ever mention Don Pham to you?"

"Never." He started for the door. Hand on the knob,

he turned back. "Do you mean you believe Rafe was working for this gangster? Have you proof?"

"He wasn't at your father's funeral. Didn't you think that was a little odd?"

"The child was ill," Hai said.

"Not so ill Carpenter couldn't come down here."

"Here?" Hai stared. "But the warehouse was closed."

"I saw him. He met a man off a power launch, and gave him two attaché cases. Do you know what was in those cases?"

"No, I do not." Hai was indignant. "What sort of man?"

"An Asian, stocky build, well-dressed. I thought it might be Don Pham, but I was too far away to be sure."

"This is incredible." Hai sat down in his desk chair again, hands to his head. "What do you think was going on? We haven't had any thefts. Not for months."

"What about drugs?" Dave said. "Suppose Don Pham has arranged for drugs to be brought over here from the Golden Triangle concealed in your crates of stereos and VCRs?"

"Impossible." Hai held hands up, palms outward. "Customs would have discovered it." He snatched up the telephone on the desk. "We will get Rafe up here to explain."

Dave took the receiver from him and put it back. "Not now, please. It's not Rafe I'm after. It's Don Pham. And I don't want Don Pham to know that. Not yet."

"You think it was he who killed my father?" Pain flickered in his face. "How I wish I had insisted on going with him that night." He struck a fist on the desk.

"Pham has a crew of little thugs in black who carry machine guns to do his killing for him. A witness saw two of them at the marina near the time of your father's death."

"My father was killed with a small pistol," Hai said.

"They didn't have their Uzis that night," Dave said. "Maybe to make your father's murder look different from the slaughter at the Hoang Pho restaurant."

Hai's eyes opened wide for a second. He said something, but not in English. He was pale, and when he stood up he did it shakily. "I must go now. Busy day, busy day." He headed again for the door.

Dave said, "Were the men killed at the Hoang Pho friends of your father's?"

"No." He yanked the door open. "We knew nothing about that. Nothing." And he was off, hurrying between the busy desks of his clerical staff, bursting out the main office door, and almost running away along the rattly catwalk.

"He'll tell Rafe Carpenter what you saw," Tracy Davis said. She sat across the table from Dave at a Newport Marina restaurant. Beside the table wide plate glass let them look across a plank deck at glossy white pleasure craft moored in long rows. The water was calm, and reflected the flame colors of the sky at sunset. She poked around in a big salad, looking for any chunks of crabmeat she might have missed. She gave up, laid her fork down, took another sip of margarita from a bowl-size stem glass. She looked at Dave through those green framed glasses. "He'll tell him you've got his bank records."

Dave polished off the last of a plateful of scallops sautéed in brown butter. "I sincerely hope so." He touched his mouth with a napkin, laid the napkin beside his plate, and gave her a smile. "That was the idea."

"It's dangerous," she said. "You said you were fed up with being shot at. Now look what you've done. Set yourself up to be murdered like Mr. Le."

"Not quite." Dave took cigarettes from his jacket

pocket. He held out the pack to Tracy Davis, she took a cigarette. With a slim steel lighter, he lit it for her, lit his own. "Mr. Le didn't know it was coming."

"We ought to tell Lieutenant Flores," she said. Flores was in charge of the Le murder investigation. "Turn the papers over to him, let him handle it."

Dave said, "It's too early. The papers don't tie Carpenter to Le's murder. And I can only guess the meaning of what I saw on the docks yesterday." He smiled at her worried freckled face. "If he's up to no good, and he knows I'm on his trail, he'll try to find out what I know, won't he?" A blond young waiter in white shorts, white shirt, white socks, white deck shoes, poured coffee for them, asked if their meal had been all right, and went away. "He'll come to me. Maybe after that we can go to Flores."

"What if it's what you think?" she said. "That he's handling Don Pham's drug import operation under cover of working in Le's warehouse? Why won't he tell Don Pham you're onto him? Why won't it be Don Pham who comes to you?"

Dave shook the idea off. "Carpenter wouldn't be so stupid. You only have to meet Don Pham once to know he isn't the type who gives anyone a second chance. No—Don Pham would be the last person Carpenter would tell."

"I hope so," Tracy Davis said glumly. She tore open a little paper packet of sugar and emptied it into her coffee. She poured cream into the coffee, found her spoon, stirred the coffee. She glanced up at him. Solemnly. "He gave you a second chance."

"Yup." Dave tasted his own coffee. "And that puzzled me until I had time to think about it."

Tracy Davis put out her cigarette. "Why did he?"

The boy in white picked up their plates. Dave asked

him to bring brandies. Dave said to Tracy Davis, "Why did you come to me?"

She blinked surprise. "Why did I—?" She was indignant. "Are you comparing me with that—that—?"

"You had a use for me," Dave said. "And so did he."

She stared. "What use?"

Dave shrugged. "He didn't say, did he? So, all I can do is what I always do in the way I always do it. For you. For that half-brother you bad-mouth so often it has to mean you love him." Dave gave her the corner of a smile. "That's what you want. What Don Pham wants, I don't know. He thinks I don't need to know. But you and he are alike in this—you don't believe I'm going to deliver."

"What if you can't?" she said. The boy set snifters of brandy on the table. Tracy picked hers up and moved it round and round, watching it moodily. "What if you fail him?"

"He's a man who can't afford mistakes," Dave said. "And he doesn't think I'm going to fail him." He lifted his glass and gave her a smile. "Why don't we drink to that?"

She fretted. "I can't believe he expected you to nail him for drug smuggling. How would that suit his plans?"

Dave cocked an eyebrow, shook his head. "Damned if I know." He tossed back the brandy. "We'll see, won't we?"

10

He followed streams of red tail lights inland from the coast along miles of broad clean freeway. Before he reached it, a glow in the sky above the hills told him the shopping center was there. A spur of fresh black tarmac curved upward between hills, and when he got to the top, the shopping center sprawled bright below him. Five minutes later, he swung into a vast parking lot landscaped with slender young trees, and crowded with cars, waxed finishes reflecting rainbows from a riot of neon signs.

Show-windowed shops framed the lot on three sides—women's wear, beauty parlors, toy stores, book and record shops, jewelers, auto parts suppliers, furniture salesrooms, restaurants of many kinds. The American ones boasted steaks grilled over mesquite fires, barbecued ribs, New York bagels, Boston scrod, New Orleans crab, Maine lobster. There was a fake London fish and chips shop. There were Italian places, French,

Chinese, Korean, Japanese, West African. He worked his way toward Madame Le's Pearl of Saigon.

Inside, the place was a far cry from the cool pastels and hard plastic surfaces of the Hoang Pho. Madame Le had chosen Far East motifs—carved screens, cinnabar and black lacquer, rattan furniture, heavy bamboo beams, palm-leaf roofing, slow-turning ceiling fans, the Joseph Conrad, Somerset Naugham, Graham Greene look. Shadows. Mystery. Intrigue. The spicy food smells perfuming the air were no different from those of the Hoang Pho. The tiny young woman who led him to a table in a sheltered booth was like the one at Hoang Pho. So were the other waitresses and waiters, young, slight, black hair, black eyes, skin smooth as ivory. He ordered brandy and coffee and asked:

"Is Mr. Fergusson here tonight?"

She blinked, looked at him warily, "You want to see Mr. Fergusson?"

"Please," Dave said. She glanced off someplace, undecided, and he dug out the folder and opened it so she could see his license. "I'm with the Public Defender's office. I need to talk to him about the death of Mr. Le Van Minh."

"Ah." Dave's official standing made her brows twitch. She dipped her head. "I will speak to him." She scurried away. Silver clinked softly on china, glassware tinkled, voices murmured around him in soft rosy light. In a few minutes, the tiny young woman came back with his brandy and coffee and, seeing that he was smoking, fetched him a bulky soapstone ashtray carved with dragons. "Mr. Fergusson be here soon." With another frightened nod she vanished.

It wasn't exactly soon. Dave had time to finish the cigarette, drink half his coffee, half his brandy, and light another cigarette. He pushed back a jacket cuff to see his watch, and when he looked up Fergusson was standing there, young, yellow-haired, rosy-cheeked, blue-eyed, a little sweaty, and giving off kitchen smells. He had got out of an apron and into his jacket hurriedly. Its collar was turned up at the back. One shirt collar point stuck out.

"I'm Fergusson," he said, "what can I do for you?"

Dave introduced himself and said, "Sit down. Tell me about the night your father-in-law was killed."

"I told it all to the police," Fergusson said. "As you can see, we're very busy tonight. Can't this wait?"

"The police report says you were here at the restaurant, working on accounts." Dave nodded at the bench opposite him. Fergusson gave an impatient look around him at his domain and with a sharp sigh sat down. On the seat's edge. He didn't relax. "Until midnight. But alone. You have no witness."

"What's wrong?" Fergusson scowled. "The police have Andy Flanagan in jail. It's an open and shut case."

"The Public Defender doesn't think so," Dave said.

"Well, I certainly didn't do it." He laughed—not a happy laugh, an angry laugh. "You think I killed Mr. Le? That's crazy. He's done more for me than—You're crazy."

"Normally, at that time of night, you'd have been at the Le house with your wife and children, and all the Le's, isn't that right? You enjoy living there?"

"Of course. They're the only family I ever had. I love them, they love me. What are you saying?"

"Your brother-in-law, Hai, said he argued with his father, tried to keep him from leaving the house in response to Andy Flanagan's phone call. Why?"

"Come on," Fergusson taunted. "Have you seen the Old Fleet Marina? That whole district? It's not safe."

"Yet Mr. Le insisted on taking nearly six thousand dollars in cash with him."

"Hai was right. He should have gone along."

"He looks strong to me. And Mr. Le was frail, isn't that so? Couldn't Hai have had his way if he really tried?"

Fergusson shook his head sharply. "You don't understand. It's a question of custom, the way they do things back in Vietnam. Mr. Le was head of the family, the father, and his word was law. You're not there to question his decisions. You're there to obey. Oh, it's one thing if he asks your opinion. But if he doesn't, you don't offer it. He was going to meet Flanagan and try to ease things for the people being dislocated—that's what the cash was for.

"He pictured himself going around like Santa Claus handing out money to the boaties who needed it most. It was a bad idea, because it wasn't enough—anyone could see that. Hell, there were ninety of them. Are. How far was six thousand going to go? And if he did give a few of them enough to really help, then the others would be all over him. There'd be no end to it."

Fergusson's shoulders sagged, he sat back in the chair, reached for Dave's cigarette pack, took a cigarette from it, lit it with Dave's lighter. "Thanks. It was a spur-of-the-moment reaction Mr. Le was having. Angry. And guilty. He wanted to shut Flanagan and the rest of them up. He didn't like the bad publicity. He'd donated to good causes for years in the Vietnamese community. He didn't like being made out a villain in the newspapers and on TV. He felt he had the right to sell what belonged to him, but he also felt sorry for the boaties. That was why he'd let them stay on way past the deadline."

"And now he thought he'd buy them off," Dave said.

Fergusson nodded wearily. "He wasn't thinking clearly. He could be hot-headed. It was late. The call had woken him up. If it was morning, he'd never have tried it." Fergusson sat forward, twisted out the cigarette, started to rise. "I have to get back to the kitchen. Short-handed tonight. Cooks always call in sick when it's busiest."

"Wait another minute," Dave said. "I need to know two things, maybe three. First about Ba's death."

"Oh, Jesus," Fergusson moaned. "We'll none of us get over that. It's so—incomprehensible." He spread his hands in a gesture of helplessness. "He was healthy as I am. Young, lightweight but wiry. And one night he goes to bed and just dies there. It's weird. But it happens to young South Asian men. And medicine doesn't have an inkling, not really. Stress, they say."

"He wanted to be a poet," Dave said. "Instead, his father made him work at the warehouse. I guess that might have caused stress. The young think these situations are never going to end, you know."

"Yeah," Fergusson nodded. Grudgingly. "Maybe you're right. But he was a happy kid. He saw things differently from you and me—he could find little bits of beauty everywhere, point this out to you, that—a patch of paint peeling off a wall, the color of a leaf crushed in the street. He . . ."—Fergusson rubbed his mouth, frowning, hunting for words—"Life was full of beautiful surprises to him. It was so damned sad for somebody like that to die."

"There wasn't an autopsy," Dave said. "Why not?"

"Old Mrs. Le," Fergusson said. "Ba's grandmother—she's a Buddhist. They don't believe in cutting up bodies after death. And if Le Van Minh ran the rest of us, she ran him." He squinted. "An autopsy?"

"First, four prominent Vietnamese businessmen are murdered at the Hoang Pho restaurant. Then young Ba dies in his sleep. Then Le Van Minh is murdered at the Old Fleet Marina. All of these deaths within a few weeks of each other. Why should one be an accident?"

"Why should they connect?" Fergusson said.

Dave said, "You tell me. Did your father-in-law know Mr. Phat and the others at the Hoang Pho?"

"Of course. It's a very tight community, the rich Vietmanese. He sat on committees with them. They ate dinner at each other's houses." Fergusson gave a little shudder. "He might have been with them that night, easy as not."

Dave frowned. "Why do you think Le Tran Hai told me his father didn't know those men?"

"Did he? Jesus, I can't explain that. He's smart. He'd know the police could look at his father's Rolodex and find Phat and those others listed there. I never knew Hai to lie to anybody."

Dave smiled faintly. "I alarmed him today. He was flustered—that must be the reason." Dave went on to tell Fergusson of his noon visit to the warehouse on the pier. And of his earlier visit, after the funeral. And a little about Don Pham and the doll-boys. "They were watching your father. Don Pham says they didn't kill him, but they were at the Old Fleet at the time he died—a witness told me so. I think they meant to kill him. Why?"

"Dope smuggling?" Fergusson's face twisted as he argued in his mind with the idea. "No. If old Mr. Le knew about it he'd have put a stop to it at once. Same for Hai." He shook his head, stubborn with conviction. "No way would either of them have had anything to do with anything crooked. As for Rafe Carpenter, he and his wife and boy were at the house once for dinner, but I don't know him that well. All I know is, Mr. Le trusted him."

"So Hai told me," Dave said wryly. "That's sometimes a flaw in trustworthy people—they're too trusting of others."

Fergusson bristled. "You don't know for sure what

Carpenter was doing at the pier that day. No drugs were ever discovered in any of the Le cargoes."

"So Hai said. And I believe he believes that. If only because he's the one adult male member of the Le clan still alive. I wonder how long that will last."

Fergusson paled and stumbled up out of his chair. "You mean he's in danger? Have you told the police? Is anybody protecting him?"

"He's not in danger yet."

"How can you know that?" Fergusson's voice cracked.

"Sit down. Relax. Here's what's been happening today. First of all, at some point, after thinking about it, Hai braced Rafe with what I'd told him, with the evidence I'd shown him."

"Oh, my God," Fergusson wailed.

Dave held up a hand. "Don't get excited. There's a killer in the picture—we both know that. But I doubt it's Carpenter. He's only a bag man—he delivers the contraband, gets the payoff, and delivers that. I don't think he's going to run and tell Don Pham or whoever pays him that he got caught red-handed. But he's scared, and run he will. And when he does, I believe he'll run to me."

"You're awfully sure of yourself," Fergusson grouched. "Why hasn't Hai turned him over to the law by now?"

"You know better than that. Hai would lose face."

Fergusson sighed. "Yeah, you're right. Even though the Les had nothing to do with it, they should have prevented it—that's how Hai will see it. It's how the old man would have seen it. They shouldn't have let it happen, and they did, and the name Le would be disgraced forever." He twisted out his cigarette in the soapstone bowl. "What will you do when Carpenter comes to you?"

"Get him to tell me who his boss is."

Fergusson's eyebrows rose. "Just like that?" He snapped his fingers. "Why would he do that?"

"Because if this is as big a case as I think it is, if he turns state's evidence he won't have to go to jail. The Justice Department will protect him under their hide-the-witness-protection program. Relocate him and his family under a new identity. He has everything to gain and nothing to lose. My attorney can arrange it with a couple of phone calls. Carpenter will tell me." Dave drank some brandy. "Now, you tell me about your beautiful visitor—Thao."

"What?" Fergusson's jaw dropped. He knocked a fork off the table, picked it up. "What do you know about her?"

"Nothing"—Dave smiled—"that's why I'm asking."

"She's the daughter of an old friend and benefactor of Mr. Le—Nguyen Dinh Thuc, a cabinet minister in the last administration at Saigon before the Commies took over. Wealthy businessman—in exile in France, now. He lent Mr. Le the money to start over in the States. But Washington says Nguyen made off with unauthorized U.S. funds, and if he enters this country, they'll nail him." Fergusson kept fidling with the fork, looking at everything but Dave. "So he sent Thao. She'll be going home soon." He sounded relieved.

"At the funeral," Dave said, "she seemed awfully upset."

"Yeah, well—" Fergusson cleared his throat. "She's kind of Westernized, you know?" He twitched a feeble smile. "She doesn't hold her emotions in like most Asians do, or try to. She's more French than Vietnamese, really."

"It's a long way to come just to say hello," Dave said.

"Yeah." Fergusson stood up. "Look, I have to get back to work." He surveyed the busy room. "People are waiting for their food."

"Am I right," Dave asked, "that we've met before?"

Fergusson gulped, shook his head. "No. I don't think so. Excuse me, please." And he rushed off.

"Oh, yes we have," Dave said softly. But where, when?

"For Christ sake," Cecil said, "where have you been? I've been calling all over Southern California. You were going to phone me at home."

In the dim black-and-silver-papered hallway leading to the restrooms of Madame Le's Saigon, where a mute row of shiny pay telephones waited, Dave read his watch. "I'm sorry. It's been one damned thing after another."

"Numbers just about worn off the push-buttons here," Cecil said. "I ran out of ideas after a while. Tried to get that Tracy Davis half a dozen times. Out of the office. Was she with you?"

"It's not a romance," Dave said. "Just business."

"You had dinner with her, right?"

"To bring her up to date on the case," Dave said. "You can't be jealous. Why were you calling?"

"Because a man kept calling you. Ralph Carpenter?"

"I'll bet," Dave said. "But it's Rafe, not Ralph."

"Yeah, well, whatever. I said for him to call back, and he sure as hell did, time after time. And the last time I was going out the door to come here to earn my grits and greens, and I figured I'd hear from you, and so I said for him to leave a number where you could reach him, and I'd pass it to you when you called me. But he didn't want to do that, so he kept calling me here. Donaldson loved that. He expects me to do a little work once in a while, not keep trying to calm down hysterical strangers on the telephone."

"What did Carpenter say he wanted, exactly?"

"Nothing exact about it, except the last call, an hour ago, he said if you called, I was to tell you to meet him at Pier Nine at eleven, the Le warehouse. Alone."

"Ah, that's more like it." Dave grinned to himself. "Just the news I've been waiting to hear."

"Sounds dangerous to me. Who is this dude?"

Dave told him. "If I'm right, his boss is Don Pham. Don't tell me you wouldn't like to see Don Pham locked up."

"Don't go there, Dave. You know those docks at night. Why should this Carpenter tell you anything? Why won't he just kill you? Even if Hai guessed what happened, he'd keep quiet to save face. You'd be dead for nothing. What would I do, then? Shit, you don't even have your gun."

Dave groaned. "It's at Mel Fleischer's." Cecil was right—he shouldn't go alone, certainly not unarmed. "Look, can you get out of there? Go to Mel's, pick up the Sig-Sauer. And meet me at the real estate office on the waterfront." He read his watch again. "If you start now, you'll just have time."

"I would if I had a helicopter," Cecil said. "You wait, hear me? Don't do anything till I get there."

11

The waterfront was as deserted and, except for the wash of water against the sea wall, as silent as if the world had ended. Dave had parked the Jaguar up a side street as before and gone on foot along the walk that faced the docks. The lights on the docks were spaced far apart. Out in the harbor, the sparse lights of anchored freighters and tankers only hinted their dark shapes, their hulking size. Reflections of the lights wavered yellow, red, green in the black water.

He stationed himself well back in the shadowed entryway of the real estate place. Cold wind blew off the water. Blown trash, fried chicken bones, hot dog wrappers, soft drink cups crackled under his shoes. He peered at his watch. Ten forty. A light burned above the door of the Le warehouse. He saw it through the iron tracery of the crane whose lofty top was lost in high darkness. The light outlined stacks of empty crates on the dock.

He waited. He wanted a cigarette but he didn't light one. Invisibility might be important. This kind of waiting he had mastered long ago. Everybody in his line of work learned it after a while. Tension had no part in it. Tension tired you out. Excitement? Excitement made you make mistakes. All you wanted was a certainty that something would happen when it happened. This made for a kind of ease that came close to sleep but wasn't sleep. Your thoughts could wash around one small, focused point of concentration, like surf around a rock, until the moment came to move.

His point of focus was the pair of chain-link gates that let traffic down onto the pier. Unless something had happened to him, in the next twenty minutes Rafe Carpenter would drive up in that shiny car, leave it for a few seconds to work the padlock and swing the gates open, get back into it and drive it down the long ramp. Would he stop it there, come back, lock the gates again, to make sure Dave came to him on foot? Dave didn't like the thought. He hadn't believed Carpenter was danger-ous. But desperation could change people.

At five minutes before eleven he began to listen in the water-lapping hush for Carpenter's car. Or Cecil's van. Or both. He didn't hear the engine of a car, tires on grit, the ratcheting of a parking brake, but he heard car doors close quietly. Not out here on the waterfront, some-where back behind the row of shops. Not Cecil's—he knew the sound of those doors. Carpenter's car? Not back there. Why more than one door? He strained to hear voices, footfalls. He heard nothing. He took two steps, inched his head out of the entryway, and peered along the street, to his right, to his left. Not a sign of life. He pulled his head in, waited a half minute, and looked again. Nothing. He stepped back into deep shadow and waited.

Not forever. For ten minutes. Then he decided Carpenter must have got here before him. Or had been here for hours. Why wasn't it from here he'd made that last phone call to Cecil at the television station? Why else ask Dave to meet him here? Dave stepped out of the doorway, again looking quickly along the waterfront street, left, right. Maybe a figure, small, slim, black-clad, flitted out of sight a few shops along. Maybe he imagined it. He didn't think so. Once, twenty years ago, ten years ago, maybe even five, he'd have gone to look. Tonight, he didn't go.

But he didn't wait for the gun either. He crossed the sand-strewn asphalt of the street, went down the zigzag plank staircase to the pier, walked out the pier, heading for the Le warehouse. The sound of the water lapping the sea wall, the barnacled pier stakes was louder here, but he thought he still might catch the noise of Cecil's van if it arrived. Then the diesel of one of the anchored ships started, its rough basso thrum sounding in his ears like the coursing of his own blood through his veins. Soon this was joined by the clatter of an anchor chain, the howl of the rusty donkey engine lifting it. Shouted orders and replies in a strange language came over the water, the noise of hurrying footsteps on steel plates. The ship's whistle bellowed, echoing and re-echoing off the surrounding warehouses.

Dave hadn't seen Carpenter's car because it was parked behind a stack of crates. He peered at it. No one sat inside. He went straight to the small door set in the big doors of the warehouse. He tried the door. It was locked. He drew back a fist to bang on it, and the ship's whistle roared again. The sound was like a physical blow. He waited for the echoes to quit, then hammered on the warehouse door. The noise of his pounding ricocheted through the place. He waited for results. A full minute.

He banged on the door again, waited again, another full minute. And it came to him that no one was in there. This was only instinct, but many times in a long, hazardous life his instincts had proved out. So where was Rafe Carpenter. He stepped back.

"Carpenter." His shout banged off the front of the warehouse, off the dark water, the sides of ships. Nobody answered. "Carpenter? It's Brandstetter." Still there was only the lap of the water and the fading thump-thump-thump of the freighter's diesel as it hove down the harbor for the open sea. "Carpenter?" Silence. Not a nice silence. The man's car was here. The man had to be here. Dave stepped to the door, pounded on it again, shouted the name again. Nothing. He tried again to open the door. No use.

He turned away, and again thought he saw a flitting figure. Out of the corner of his eye. Up at the land end of the pier. He stopped in his tracks and squinted hard up at the feebly lit wharf. Could it be Cecil? No. He wouldn't dodge out of sight that way. It had to be one of Don Pham's doll-boys, didn't it? Dressed in black, small, slim, moving like a shadow, silent as a shadow? For a second, he felt fear.

Then he laughed at himself. If they'd killed Rafe Carpenter, they wouldn't still be hanging around. If they'd come to kill Dave, they could have done it in the doorway of the real estate shop. No—they were following him to find out what he found out, weren't they? And he'd found out nothing. So they'd wasted their time. Good. He frowned again at the warehouse door. Had Carpenter glimpsed the doll-boys too? Was he too scared of them to show himself? It made sense, but Dave's instincts said Carpenter just plain wasn't in the warehouse. So where was he? "Carpenter?" he called again, and began to walk back up the pier.

A creak and a wiry snarl overhead warned him. A voice shouted, "Dave, look out!" Someone hit him in a flying tackle and, locked in the tackler's grip, he rolled across the wharf. A mighty weight struck the wharf and shook it. Wood splintered, nails shrieked. There was a jangle of metal and glass. A light machine gun chattered. He was in the water, under the water, water that tasted of diesel fuel. His clothes were heavy. He pumped his arms hard, but rose to the surface slowly. He coughed air into his lungs, wiped a hand down over his face, pushed hair out of his eyes. Cecil bobbed in the water too, a yard away, spitting water, scowling at him. "I said for you to wait. Couldn't you just once do what I say?"

"Next time," Dave gasped. "How do we get out of here?"

"Catalina Island might be safe," Cecil said.

They waited for a few minutes, treading water under the pier. Nothing happened, and they climbed back up to the wharf by a crude ladder hung with coarse black seaweed, rungs nailed to a splintery pier. The wind felt cold. They shivered in their wet clothes. A giant crate lay smashed on its heavy net. It had held stereo receivers. The remains of these glittered everywhere. Transistors and micro chips crunched under their shoes. Cecil pointed to the shadowy top of the crane. "Somebody was up there. He made a little noise. I looked up, saw him just in time."

Dave said, "For me." Kicking aside shiny metal plates, knobs, switches, he walked to the foot of the crane where great bolts anchored it to a foot-thick concrete base. A man lay there, very still, one leg bent under him in a way only possible for the dead. "Not in time for him."

Cecil came up beside him. "Is it Carpenter?"

Dave nodded. "I was wondering where he was."

Cecil knelt beside the body. "He didn't just fall," he said. "He was shot. Time after time."

"You're not the only one looking out for me," Dave said.

Cecil squinted up at him. "Don Pham?"

"His Ninjas." Dave nodded at Carpenter's corpse. "Get his keys for me." Cecil found them, stood, handed them to him. "Thank you," Dave said, "and for saving my life. Again." He put the keys into a pocket, gave Cecil a kiss, a one-armed hug. Water from Cecil's sleeve oozed between his fingers, cold as the grave. He shuddered inside himself, and pulled the hand away. "Let's find a phone," he said.

Stripped of their wet clothes, and wrapped in police-issue blankets, a blue one, a khaki-colored one, they sat in the back of a Harbor Police car. Not handcuffed, but not exactly free, either. The rear door of the car was open. Lieutenant Raoul Flores, a thick man of forty, stood outside, hands on the car's roof, leaning in at them. His skin was the smooth brown of a fine Aztec pot. His eyes were small and black and without humor. His white strong teeth would have served a smile well. But Flores didn't smile. Not tonight. He said grimly, "This should not be news to me, Mr. Brandstetter. I should have been told about all of this."

Tracy Davis stood beside him. "That was my fault, Lieutenant. I was going to tell you tomorrow."

"It was your fault, and it was Mr. Brandstetter's fault, and it is not something I can lightly dismiss. An apology is not enough."

A gurney passed, small wheels bumping over the wharf's rough planks, mincing the glass fragments. White-clad ambulance attendants pushed the gurney towards a van with open rear doors, lights on the roof turning round and round, red, amber, white. It stood among four more police cars on the wharf, doors also open, radio speakers crackling now and then with the staticky code words of a female police dispatcher. Uniformed men, men out of uniform, prowled the pier with flashlights. Two clambered around high up on the crane. In the bright open doorway of the warehouse, a bald plainclothes man talked to Le Tran Hai and made jottings in a notebook. Hai looked grumpy. He was without a necktie. His hair was tousled from sleep. Flores lit a Mexican cigarette. The sharp sweetness of its smoke brought back memories to Dave of boyhood trips to Baja with his father fifty years ago. Flores pointed at the gurney.

"That man would be alive now, if you had come to me with your information when you were supposed to."

"It wasn't hard evidence," Dave said.

"He tried to kill you." Flores's tone was rich with sarcasm. "And somebody killed him. I find it difficult to believe these things happened because he was a saint."

"What we had didn't prove any wrongdoing," Dave said.

"You saw him meet and pay off a drug smuggler down here the day of Mr. Le's funeral," Flores said.

"You're upset, and I don't blame you, but you mustn't let it interfere with your thinking," Dave said. "I saw him meet a man off a power launch and give the man two attaché cases. I don't know who the man was. I don't know what was in the cases."

"You got his bank records," Flores said. "He was banking money he never earned, spending money he never earned."

"But Le Tran Hai says it couldn't have been from smuggling. All their shipments are inspected. Customs haven't turned up any drugs."

"Then Carpenter was ripping off inventory," Flores said. "It's the commonest sort of crime on the docks, you know that. So common they don't even bother to report it when and if they discover it. And smart thieves, working inside a place, the way Carpenter did for the Les—they make changes in the bills of lading. It can go on for years."

Dave shrugged. The blanket slipped from his shoulders. He felt cold and pulled it back up. "Did Le Tran Hai call you after I showed him those bank records of Carpenter's?"

Flores snorted in disgust. "You know the damn Vietnamese. Would they admit it if a crime was committed by an employee? Hell no. He won't admit tonight what happened here was anything but an accident. It's some crazy chink code of honor. Was it Don Pham"— Flores liked changing subjects abruptly—"Carpenter met here that day?"

"Maybe," Dave said, "maybe not. He was too far away."

"But you think I'm wrong, holding Andy Flanagan for the murder of Le Van Minh. You think Don Pham was behind it?"

"I think he was behind the killing of Phat, Tang, and the other Vietnamese businessmen at the Hoang Pho. I have a witness who saw the same little gangster types there as came to my house with Pham the other night, and tonight so obligingly shot Rafe Carpenter."

"What witness? Why haven't I talked to him?"

"You have. He doesn't trust the police."

"But he trusted you? I want to talk to him."

"He's in New York, and he doesn't plan to come back."

Flores's eyes narrowed. "Who do you mean—that black faggot dishwasher? He claimed he hid in a trash module in the alley, and saw nothing."

Cecil drew an angry breath, and Dave said quickly, "Lieutenant, let's stick to the subject. I figured Le's murder was a leftover from the Hoang Pho killings, so Don Pham was responsible for it too. But he denies that, and I believe him."

"Why—is he a friend of yours?" Flores said. "He told you he deals drugs, isn't that what you said?"

"No—the weapon was wrong. Yes, he told me he deals drugs, but that may just have been bragging. If he dealt drugs, you'd know it, and you'd have him in jail for it by now, isn't that right?"

"I know he deals drugs," Flores said drily. "Getting him into jail for it is something else. If he isn't your friend, why are his boys bodyguarding you?"

Dave grunted. "I'm not sure they were his boys. I didn't get a good look. But if they were, the honest to God truth is, Lieutenant, I don't know why."

"Come on, Brandstetter. When Tracy here hired you, I went to the library and read up on you in magazines. And nobody ever wrote anyplace that you were stupid."

"They also never wrote I was a mind-reader," Dave said. "Don Pham wants something from me. I'd bet on that. But I don't know what it is."

"No idea?" Flores said. "No idea at all?"

"Possibly it connects to the Le family. Pham knew I'd never let him hire me to investigate them, so he pointed me that way, and set his boys to follow me."

"And when you turn up what he wants, they will hustle you into a car and take you to Don Pham so you can tell him, and after that, they will no longer be your bodyguards, will they?" Flores said. "They will be your executioners. They enjoy that. They do it well. Again and again."

"Don't talk like that," Tracy Davis cried.

Flores pulled his head out of the car and looked at her in exaggerated surprise. "Ah, counselor—you are a woman, after all." He gave a short, sharp laugh, took a last drag on the Mexican cigarette, and flicked it away in a long arc. He watched its little red spark wink out in the dark water. He said to Tracy Davis, "You may well worry. You brought him into this. His death will be on your head."

"Don't listen to him, Tracy," Dave said. And to Flores, "What point would there be in killing me?"

"You are joking," Flores said. "Don Pham will act on the information you gather for him. And if you are still living when he does this, you will know who was behind it. And as a man of honor, you will tell the authorities, and Don Pham will go to prison. Simple, no?" Flores leaned into the car again, and said to Cecil, "Mister Television Reporter, why don't you save the life of your friend one more time tonight? Drive him home and make him stay there." His terra cotta face was close to Dave's, his warm breath cloying from the tobacco. "Go home, *viejo*. Let us young dudes have a chance, okay?" Now he did smile, but it hadn't been worth waiting for. It looked like a snarl. "Trust us. We can do the job. It is what the citizens pay us for."

"They also pay you"—Dave sneezed—"to shut down illegal gambling establishments." He sneezed again. And a third time. "To get prostitutes off the streets, and"—he sneezed and shivered and wiped his nose on a corner of the blanket because there was nothing else for the purpose—"and to lock up drug pushers." He blinked watery eyes at Flores, and smiled. "I think you need all the help you can get."

Flores sighed grimly, slammed the door shut, walked around, got into the car behind the steering wheel, and slammed that door. He started the engine. It sounded as if it didn't have many miles left in it. "I will take you to your car. Where did you say you parked it?"

* * *

Cecil knocked nails into the bookshelves that flanked the fireplace, strung a cord between the nails, and hung their wet clothes on the cord to dry. He was naked and, moving lean and lithe in the flickering orange light of the fire in the grate, looked like the First Man, home from the hunt. Dave, just out of a hot shower, stood drying his hair in the bathroom doorway, and watched him. He ached, his nose ran, he was getting a sore throat, but what he saw made him smile. He got into blue warm-up pants, pulled up the hood of a blue warm-up top, and tied the strings. He went toward the bar that lurked in shadow at the far end of the long room.

"Hold it," Cecil said. "Wait for the pot to boil."

"What are you talking about?" Dave turned and grinned at him. "By the way, Emperor, I love your new clothes."

"Thank you," Cecil said. He moved out of the firelight, headed for the door. "If you want to lose that cold, I have the answer." He pulled the door open, and went out into the dark courtyard, the lights of the cook shack yellow on its far side. "Drink nothing," he called back, "till you hear from me." Laughing, shaking his head, Dave sat on the couch. Cecil could go naked if he wanted to. No one was likely to see and be shocked at two-thirty in the morning. And up here in the canyon, miles from the sea, the night was not cold. He was cold. And bruised, from that roll across the dock. His ribs hurt where Cecil had hit him in that flying tackle. He touched the place and winced. But cracked ribs had their point, particularly when he considered the alternative. He sat and watched flames licking a shag-barked eucalyptus log. Sea water dripped from the hanging clothes onto the raised brick hearth. Monotonously. He fell asleep. Cecil said, "Now then—ready for Dr. Harris's magical mystery cure?"

"Huh?" Dave jerked awake. Cecil stood over him, holding a big tray of Mexican hammered tin. He set this on an end table under a lamp and switched on the lamp. A thick water tumbler was on the tray, what looked like two jiggers of whisky in it. A tea strainer. A long-handled spoon. A jar of honey. A lemon cut in half. And the yellow enamel Japanese kettle from the cookstove, steam wisping from its spout. Dave blinked. "What's all this?"

"Show and tell time." Cecil knelt, rubbing his hands together eagerly. "Watch carefully, and in years to come, when Mother is no longer here to nurse you through your little sicknesses, you can do this for yourself."

Dave laughed. "Mother is an idiot," he said.

Cecil grinned. "But she loves you, don't forget that." He held the tea strainer over the tumbler and squeezed the juice from the two halves of lemon through it into the whisky. He used the spoon to stir the mixture. Next he unscrewed the lid of the honey jar, plunged the spoon into the honey, cranked the spoon around and brought it out, clotted with honey, and put the spoon into the glass and let the honey slide off it into the whisky and lemon. Now he picked up the kettle by its wooden handle and slowly poured hot water into the tumbler, stirring with the spoon slowly, steadily. Dave's nose wasn't working well, but the smell of the concoction was strong. Heady. He leaned over the steaming tumbler and inhaled.

"It can't be medicine," he said, "it smells too good."

Cecil laughed. "Wait till you taste it." He let the spoon rattle onto the tray, stood up, made for the bathroom. "Don't drink it yet." He was back in seconds. "Hold out your hand." Dave obeyed. Cecil put aspirins into his palm. "Take those with it, climb in bed, and in the morning, you won't even remember you had a cold."

"Where would I be without you?" Dave said, and added hastily, "Don't answer that."

12

The Le house stood on a flat quarter acre carved out of a hillside with a view of the sea in the distance. The walls were white. Stands of bamboo sheltered roofs of red tiles. The roofs turned up at the corners from a walled forecourt of raked white gravel and flowering shrubs, broad shallow stairs led up to a moon gate of red lacquered lattice work into a spacious courtyard. The house itself was built around this. Terra cotta squares paved it. Banana trees and tropical plants grew leathery-leaved in corners. Golden carp swam beneath lily pads in a large pond in the center of the courtyard. Except for the rustling of the bamboo in the wind, all was silence here. It was meant to be a place away from the world, wasn't it, peaceful, well-ordered? But if there were any such places, he knew this wasn't one of them.

The young woman who had wept and anguished at Le Van Minh's funeral came from the house. Nguyen Hoa Thao. In a simple dress of undyed pongee, high-collared, fastened with small cloth buttons and loops at the throat, a dress that showed how perfectly she was made, she stood looking at him without expression. Had she noticed him at the cemetery, watching her? He couldn't be sure. She said in a low voice, "What is it? Why have you come here?"

"I've come to see you," he said. "Miss Nguyen, is it?"

She narrowed her eyes, tilted her head. "Yes? That is correct." She spoke with a French accent. She acted puzzled. "But why should you wish to see me? I do not know you, do I?"

He told her who he was, walked around the pond, showed her his license. "It's about the murder of Mr. Le Van Minh."

Nerves twitched in her porcelain face. "Ah, no. That is past now. The police. The newspapers and television. Surely there are no more questions to be asked."

He smiled gently. "What about answers?"

She stiffened. "What do you mean?"

"What exactly are you doing here, Miss Nguyen?"

"I am visiting. My father was an old friend of Mr. Le's. My father could not come. He sent me to represent him. It is merely a courtesy visit." She edged Dave a little patronizing smile. "These things are not so well understood in the Western world."

"Your father will be shocked to learn Mr. Le has died."

"He knows. I telephoned him when it happened."

"It touched you deeply, didn't it?" Dave said. "You were more upset than anyone in the family at the funeral. I don't understand that. The Les have been in this country since 1975. The Nguyens have been in Paris, isn't that right? You were only a child thirteen years old. Why did you feel so close to Mr. Le?"

Thao shook her lovely head. "Come into the house," she said. She had seen something beyond Dave's shoulder. He turned, just in time for a glimpse of the tiny, wrinkled, aristocratic old woman he'd seen coming down the church steps after Le's funeral. Her expression now seemed full of hate. Then the glass-paneled doorway in which she'd stood was empty. Thao plucked his sleeve urgently. "Please. Come into the house." She pushed a red door wide and he followed her into coolness, stillness, a smell of incense.

She closed the door, and broke the stillness by clapping her hands. In a moment, a young woman who might have waited tables at Madame Le's stood at the end of a white hallway, daylight from a window at her back. "Tea," Thao said to her. The young woman gave a quick nod and disappeared. "This way," Thao said to Dave, and led him into a long living room with windows facing the sea, filled with clear morning light. The carpets were Chinese—camel's hair with blue and rose traditional designs. The furniture was Western and comfortable, covered in handsome fabrics, cool colors. Bric-à-brac stood on low polished teak tables, bud vases, porcelain figurines, graceful some of them, some subtly comic.

And everywhere, on every surface, family photographs in silver frames, in Plexiglas boxes. Some were from the old days in Vietnam. Most were from the times since, the times in California. At the beach, at Disneyland, on snowy ski slopes in the mountains. The children were young, the children were grown, the children had children of their own—babies, toddlers, in grammar school plays, in Little League uniforms. But never a picture of Nguyen Hoa Thao.

"This is your first visit here," Dave said.

"That is true," she said, and sat demurely on a couch opposite the chair he had taken, hands folded in her lap. "My father kept hoping to be able to come himself. At last the stubbornness of your government and his own failing health persuaded him this would never happen. I am his only living child. By now, I was a grown woman. So he sent me."

"With messages for Mr. Le? Letters? Instructions?"

"Instructions?" She blurted the word before she could stop herself. Color rushed into her face. She shook her head. "Not instructions. My father did not give a man like Mr. Le instructions."

"I understand Mr. Le was in your father's debt."

She shook her head again. "No. He long ago repaid the money my father lent him in nineteen seventy-five."

"All debts aren't paid in cash," Dave said.

"I—I—" She grew angry, or pretended to. "What do you mean by these questions? You say you came here to see me. I do not understand that. The man who murdered Mr. Le is in prison. Some *clochard*, some, how you say, ragamuffin, who lived at that marina Mr. Le owned. I know nothing of this man."

"I believe that," Dave said, and smiled. The minature servant came in with a tray, which she set on the table. Thao nodded, and the girl went away. Thao picked up the handsome flower-painted pot to pour the tea. Dave said, "What I have trouble believing is that your only errand in coming here was to convey your father's friendship and respect for Mr. Le. I think he had business with Mr. Le, and he sent you to conduct that business."

She set down the teapot and handed Dave a cup of tea, steam curling on its clear amber surface. She took up her own cup. Her hand was not trembling. She sketched him a smile. "And what sort of business would that have been?"

"Business that Mr. Le's enemies didn't want transacted. Business that got Mr. Le murdered."

"Enemies? Mr. Le was upright and honest in all his dealings. He was a great benefactor of the Vietnamese community here. He was beloved. You were at the funeral. That is where I saw you. You saw how many came. The church was full. What enemies would such a man have?"

Dave shrugged. "Enemies that would first kill four men like himself, responsible, wealthy Vietnamese businessmen meeting late at night in a restaurant. And then would kill Mr. Le's favorite son, Ba. And then would kill Mr. Le himself. And last night would try to have me killed."

Her eyes showed concern for him, but her face was a mask. And her hands were still steady.

"Why did you come here, Miss Nguyen? If you tell me, maybe, just maybe, we can stop any more deaths. The death of Le Tran Hai, of Madame Le, maybe even of Le Rieng Quynh and her husband, Matt Fergusson."

At that name she gave a start, her teacup rattled in its saucer, color left her face. But all she said was, "My visit here is wholly innocent. You are imagining things. What sort of enemies are these that so trouble your mind?"

Dave tasted the tea. It was spicy and flowery. "Drug smugglers," he said. "Did you ever meet Rafe Carpenter?"

She nodded. "He was a valued assistant to Hai at the warehouse. He was shot and killed last night. Hai was terribly upset. He regarded Mr. Carpenter as a friend. He means to help Mr. Carpenter's widow and his little son."

"Then he doesn't believe Carpenter was using the Le import business as a cover to smuggle in drugs from Asia?"

Her eyes widened for a moment. "Was he?"

"I think so." He told her what he'd seen on the dock

the day of Le Van Minh's funeral. He told her about Carpenter's bank statements and what they suggested. "And Lieutenant Flores of the Harbor Police agrees with me."

"Hai said nothing of this. Not in my presence."

Dave drank some more of the splendid tea. Outside somewhere small children laughed. A ball bounced. "How did you happen to meet Carpenter?"

"He came once to dinner with his family. And occasionally he stopped by during the day with Ba, to settle questions of business with the elder Mr. Le."

"So he knew the layout of this house, did he?"

She looked puzzled—"Qu'est-ce que c'est 'layout'?"

Dave gestured. "The arrangement of the rooms."

She made a move. "I do not know. I suppose so."

"Do they all open off the center compound? Every apartment with its separate entrance?"

She nodded. "Almost all, yes."

"He and Ba were friendly, were they?"

"Of course, why not?" She smiled wanly. "Everyone loved Ba. Such a dear, gentle boy. A poet." Now her face clouded. "You said a moment ago he was—murdered?"

"It seems probable to me."

"But, but he died of what they call Sudden Death Syndrome. It is a disease that kills young Southeast Asian men. The doctor showed us magazine articles. Their breathing stops in their sleep, their hearts stop beating. No one understands why. Ba had been to the doctor because of some small discomfort in his chest one day at work. But it was nothing. Then this. It was terrible." Tears trickled. She blotted them with her napkin. And suddenly she was angry again. "But what you say is far more terrible."

"It may not be true," Dave said. "But with all the other killings, it's important to know." He set down his cup and saucer and stood. "I'd like to see his room, if you'll show me, please."

She eyed him doubtfully. "For what reason?"

He smiled. "Sometimes rooms and the things in them can tell a lot about the one who lived there. More than any of us suspect." He moved off. "Is it the way he left it?"

She rose. "Nothing has changed," she said. "It was the wish of his father. He went there often, and sat for hours after Ba died. Alone."

She led Dave into the courtyard. The small children he'd seen at Le Van Minh's funeral—Oriental faces and spun-gold hair that shone in the clear morning sunlight, passed a big candy-striped beach ball between them and their pretty little mother. The ball dropped often, at which they all laughed. Now the mother—what was her name, Quynh—saw Dave and let the ball drop. It rolled into the lily pond and floated, spinning. She spoke a terse phrase to Thao, and then confronted Dave, looking up at him, solemn, urgent.

"Mr. Brandstetter? Yes. Matt described you to me. He said you believe he killed my father. Well, I wish to say to you that you are mistaken. I was with him at Madame Le's restaurant that night. He never left until we both left together to come home here. We did not go to the Old Fleet Marina. He did not kill my father."

"He told me he was alone," Dave said.

She shook her head firmly. "Only to protect me."

Dave looked at Thao. "She wasn't here?"

Thao looked at Quynh. Her face was blank. Her voice when it came was toneless. "It is as she says. Come."

She crossed the courtyard and slid open a glass panel at the front, beside the moon gate. She stepped inside, and drew the curtain back. Dave cast a glance over his shoulder. Quynh and the children had vanished. He stepped after Thao into a neat and dustless room. On the walls hung framed color photographs cut from nature magazines—odd creatures, a black and white lemur, a big-eyed tarsier, a golden frog. The bed was carefully made up, a narrow bed, with a plain beige coverlet. Books were stacked on the floor beside it. On a coffee table were a television set, a VCR, and more books. Wall shelves held a stereo, turntable, tape deck, records, video and audio tapes, books again. On a small desk under a window that framed a landscape of bamboo rested a typewriter. Beside it were strewn pages typed and scrawled over with pencil. A dictionary lay open. He picked this up. Under it was a manila folder. This he opened and found verses neatly typed—no pencil marks.

"He was making a book of his poems," Dave said.

"At the university, they encouraged him to do this," Thao said. "Ba was thirty-two, and long out of college, but his instructors there continued to be interested in his talent. They believed Ba had an important voice."

Dave laid the folder down. A page was still in the typewriter. Dave turned the platen. Words came into view. He dug reading glasses from his jacket pocket, put them on, bent to peer at the words. *Summer seems endless/The small boy as small boy/Has of course a ball/ Perhaps also a bat/An immense leather glove/Burnt with the name of a great hero/Or perhaps the small boy/ Rushes into the kitchen/Snatches cookies from a plate on the table/Drinks milk and gets milk on his chin/And laughs and chatters/But the summer is not endless/A shadow approaches/The long shadow of his father/He smiles/How can he know how cold he will grow/In this shadow/How it will keep the sun from him forever/How sad it is, this shadow/To be evil/How helpless to be anything but evil* . . . This was as far as Le Doan Ba had gotten with his poem before he lay down and died.

Dave rolled the paper out of the typewriter, folded the paper and put it into a pocket. He looked at Thao. "I'll return this later." He took off the glasses, put them away, and said, "Do you remember? Was Rafe Carpenter here, by any chance, the night Ba died?"

Frown lines appeared between her lovely brows. "Only the family," she said. "Mr. Le, Madame Le, Le Hai, Le Ba, Quynh and Matt Fergusson, the children, and the servants. We were all asleep when Ba died." She looked at the bed. "If only we had heard. The doctor said he had struggled for breath. Perhaps he cried out. But no one heard."

"And if Rafe Carpenter had come into the compound and stepped into Ba's room, no one would have heard that either, isn't that right?"

"The gate is always locked at night," she said. "No one could come in."

"Maybe Ba came out and let Carpenter in," Dave said.

"How can we know that?" She sat on the bed, smoothing the already bleakly smooth coverlet. "Ba is dead. Carpenter is dead."

"Someone knows," Dave said. "Maybe Don Pham."

She blinked. "Who?"

"A man who calls himself Don Pham. He seems to know the Le's. Was he ever at this house, that you know of?"

"No." She gave her head a firm shake. "I heard him spoken of. By Mr. Le. By Le Tran Hai. Not pleasntly. A gangster, a racketeer. The sort who give the Vietnamese in the United States a bad name. His kind was hated by this household." She eyed Dave curiously. "What a strange thing to suppose. That Don Pham would come here."

"It's my job to suppose strange things," Dave said. "Sometimes the strange things are the only ones that count." He smiled. "Like your presence here. I find that strange."

"I will be leaving soon." She gazed past him, out the window at the bamboo. She looked wistful.

"Do you miss Paris?" Dave said.

"Very much." Her smile was wan.

"Someone special? A young man?"

Color came and went in her face, she lowered her eyes. "A young man, yes." She raised her eyes, and their look defied him. Why? Because he was an old man, like her father? Standing coldly between two warm-blooded youngsters? "We are deeply in love." Chin up, she made it a declaration that challenged the world. "We care for nothing but each other. It has been hard to be apart for so long. But, of course, my father is my father, and must be obeyed in all things." She gave a little bow, whether mocking or not, Dave couldn't gauge. She sighed, and forced a smile. "How will you ever be able to find out if someone killed poor Ba?"

"Exhume the body and conduct an autopsy."

"I saw him. There were no signs of violence."

"There are ways of killing that don't leave any outward traces. That's why autopsies are necessary."

"No." The voice cracked like a whip. Startled, Thao looked toward it. So did Dave. The tiny old woman had come in. Silently. How long had she been standing there? Taking small steps, propped by a cane, she came toward him now. Thao got up to help her. She shook the girl's hand away and came on to face Dave. Fury was in her wrinkled face, arrogance in her eyes. Her voice was scratchy. She spoke Vietnamese. Sharply to Thao. Then to Dave. Thao translated. "She says there will be no autopsy. She forbade it before. She forbids it now. She forbids it forever."

"It's the law of the state of California," Dave said.

The old woman shook her head fiercely and spoke again in Vietnamese. Thao translated. "Not if the one who died had seen a doctor within twenty days of his death, and the death was from illness. And with Ba that was the way it was."

"If nobody suspected murder," Dave said, "why did that question come up?"

Thao said, "The doctor is also Vietnamese, and he suggested an autopsy because of studies he had read. Medicine does not understand this illness. He thought one more example might help solve the—how you say?—riddle."

"I see." He looked into the old woman's eyes. "And even to help keep other young men like your grandson from dying this way, you wouldn't agree?"

The old woman gabbled in her broken voice. Thao said, "It is not a decision she controls. It is sacred law. To mutilate the body of the dead is a sacrilege."

"Tell her it has to be done," Dave said. He nodded to both women and moved off. The old woman screeched after him. He didn't break his stride. He heard her cane thump the polished floor as she followed him, scolding. In the open doorway, he turned to face her, saying to Thao, "Tell her if it isn't done, if we don't prove Ba was killed and find the one who killed him, Hai could be next. She's already lost one grandson. Does she want to lose the only one left?"

"I can't tell her that," Thao said. "It's too cruel."

"Then just tell her that where the police have reason to suspect a homicide they can and will order an autopsy, and there's nothing she can do to stop it."

He walked into the courtyard and out through the moon gate. He looked up. The gate was twelve feet high, but the lattice work invited climbing. Rafe Carpenter, young and strong, could scramble over it in half a minute, and unless that room was locked at night—and why would it be?—slip inside, push a pillow down on the face of the sleeping Ba, and be gone again in next to no time. A sad shadow, for sure, and helpless to be anything but evil.

13

L e Tran Hai said, "No time, no time. Busy day." He tried to wedge his stout body past Dave's lean one in the doorway of his glass-and-steel-paneled office high at the rear of the Le warehouse. The little Vietnamese clerks stopped clicking the keyboards of their white computers and rattling fanfold printouts, and stared, interested, spectacles glinting in the hard white fluorescent light.

"This won't take long," Dave said.

"You bring trouble," Hai said.

"Other people bring it," Dave said. "I only take the wrappings off it."

"You have caused me the loss of my most trusted and valuable employee," Hai said. "If it were not for your interference, Rafe Carpenter would be alive today."

"He tried to drop a crate on me," Dave said.

"No such thing." Hai shook his head vigorously. His hair still looked uncombed. His eyes were bloodshot.

136

"That was an accident. We do not wear hardhats in our work here for nothing. The docks are dangerous."

"His hardhat didn't do Carpenter any good."

Hai barked a bitter laugh. "Ah, but you brought a different sort of danger, did you not? Guns, bullets, police."

"You're confused," Dave said. "The police had nothing to do with it. He was mixed up with drug smugglers, Mr. Le—very lethal people. They were the ones who killed him."

"You have not proved that to me, nor to the police. As to his trying to kill you—he was moving freight. Working late into the night. That is the sort of employee he was. Loyal. Devoted. No sacrifice was too much for him. He never waited to be asked. He knew what needed to be done, and he did it."

"And some of it was damned unpleasant," Dave said.

"I have just come from his home," Hai said. "You have caused terrible grief to an innocent woman, to a little boy who must now grow up without the father who loved him."

"I've just come from your home," Dave said. Hai blinked. "Where Nguyen Hoa Thao tells me you mean to see to it the widow and orphan are looked after."

"He paid for his loyalty to my father and me with his life. I must do what little I can." Hai turned away, went to his desk. A window was behind the desk. He stood staring out the window that showed gulls circling against a hard blue sky. "It is a terrible thing to lose a father."

"I agree," Dave said. "Also a brother."

Hai turned slowly, frowning. "What do you mean?"

"It never struck you as strange," Dave said, "that Ba died so short a time before your father?"

Hai squinted. "But it was illness. His heart stopped in

the night. The doctor said it was a thing that happens to some young Vietnamese men. No one understands why."

Dave sat down on a chair that faced the desk. "He'd have learned why if he'd been able to order an autopsy."

"My grandmother would not permit it."

"I know. I spoke to her this morning, too. She's a formidable lady." He smiled faintly at Hai. "But she's not in Vietnam now. She's in California. And here the law is stronger than any grandmother."

"You believe my brother was murdered?" Hai almost laughed at the idea. "But you never knew him. How could he have enemies? Le Doan Ba? He was a boy, a poet, no harm to anyone. Who would want to kill him?"

Dave took the poem out of his pocket, unfolded it, handed it across the desk to Hai. The stocky man sat down, frowned at the page. Dave watched his eyes. They took in the poem top to bottom once. Then again. He looked at Dave. "Where did you get this?"

Dave told him. "Do you understand it?"

Hai's thick hand pushed the paper away from him. He looked away. "I am a businessman," he said, "I have had no time in my life for poetry."

"Who is the boy in the poem?" Dave said.

Hai shrugged impatiently. "I am not a child. Do not ask me to play guessing games."

"Ba and Carpenter worked together here. They used to drive together to the Le house sometimes on errands to your father. They must have chatted about things. Surely Ba knew at least as much as I do about Rafe Carpenter's son. Even I know the boy is interested in baseball."

Hai scowled at the poem. "I see what you are saying. Yes. Maybe the boy in the poem is Jonno. Still—"

"And the father is Rafe Carpenter," Dave said, "and Ba wrote the poem because he'd just learned his supposed friend Rafe was up to no good here, and Ba was wondering what to do with that knowledge, how to handle it to keep Jonno from being hurt. Isn't that clear?"

Hai folded the paper and handed it back to Dave. "Nothing you bring me is ever clear, Mr. Brandstetter." He got to his feet. "I saw my brother's body after he died. It was unmarked. What do you expect an autopsy to show?"

"Tiny multiple hemorrhages in the lungs," Dave said, "indicating suffocation. I think Rafe Carpenter smothered your brother with a pillow in his bed that night."

"And later shot my father?" Hai looked scornful.

"For the same reason," Dave said. "That he was about to learn Rafe was smuggling drugs through this warehouse."

"You have no proof," Hai said. "The dead cannot speak, and poor Rafe Carpenter is dead."

"So is Ba," Dave said. "But he'll give me proof."

Tracy Davis worked among other lawyers in a honeycomb of glass cells on the eighth floor of a new county office building not far from the harbor. But her cell was empty now. A plump Latino kid, college age, wheeled a steel cart loaded with law books past her door. Dave asked him where she was. She was out to lunch. Dave rode an elevator down again, went out into sunlight glaring on the white cement of a government square planted grudgingly with young trees, and Tracy Davis came toward him, carrying a white paper sack printed with yellow arches. He waited for her on broad, shallow steps in the hot sun. When she saw him, she smiled and waved a hand, and he waved back.

"This is unexpected," she said, a little breathless from

hurrying. "I thought you'd be in bed with pneumonia today." She moved briskly on up the steps. He followed. She said, "You were starting an awful cold last night."

He made her laugh with his account of Cecil's concoction. And by the time he'd finished, they were in her office, where she sat behind the desk and opened the white sack. She took out of it a wad of paper napkins, a red and yellow box that held a hamburger, and a red paper pouch of french fries. She excused herself, went away, and came back with two mugs of coffee. The mugs were imprinted with the seal of San Pedro County. The gold was wearing off. She handed a mug to Dave, told him to sit down, sat down herself, and rummaged in a desk drawer.

"I have a letter opener here somewhere. I can cut the Big Mac in half."

"Not for me," Dave said. "Thanks. That's little enough fuel for a busy career woman." The desk was heaped with file folders, law books, blue-backed briefs, legal pads. Pencils and pens were strewn around. "I'll bet you sometimes wish you were back with Abe Greenglass."

"Sometimes." She unwrapped the hamburger and bit into it hungrily. "What's on your mind?"

He told her about his visit to the Le house, Ba's room. He took a swallow of his coffee, set the mug down, pulled the poem from his jacket pocket, and handed it across to her. She frowned, took the page, unfolded it, and read it, twice, munching steadily away at her hamburger and french fries. She looked at him blankly through her green rimmed glasses. "I was never any good at poetry. What does it mean?"

Dave reached across, took the paper, put on his reading glasses, read the poem aloud to her while she finished off her food. When he quit reading and put away his glasses, she still wasn't registering. He began to feel hopeless. He lit a cigarette and said patiently, "It's about Rafe Carpenter's little son. Ba is saying that the evil Rafe has done is going to darken and chill the boy's whole life."

"Seriously?" she said. "This is evidence?"

"Ba worked at the Le warehouse, too, remember? Why didn't he stumble across what Carpenter was doing?"

She stood, reached across, took back the poem, sat down, read it again. "I see. Right. He was wondering if he should tell his father. If he had the right to expose Carpenter and ruin a child's life."

Dave beamed at her. "See? You are good at poetry."

She handed the page back, stuffed the white sack with the red box, the red pouch, the crumpled napkins, and dropped it into a waste basket. "Unfortunately, there are no names in the document, and it isn't signed. Or dated."

"It was in the typewriter, so Ba must have written it the night he died. He couldn't finish it then—the ending would depend on what he did. And he still hadn't made up his mind. I think he'd confronted Carpenter with what he knew, Carpenter begged him not to tell, and Ba agreed at least to think about it. But Carpenter knew Ba was Vietnamese—that in the end loyalty to his father would come first."

"Obedience?" She smiled wanly.

Dave nodded. "So, after lights out at the Le house, Carpenter came and suffocated Ba. I never saw Ba, but judging by the size of the rest of the Le's, Carpenter was much bigger, much stronger. There was no autopsy. The grandmother wouldn't have it." Dave handed the folded poem back to her. "Keep it. We need an exhumation order on the body of Le Doan Ba, Tracy. If he was murdered, then there's a solid chance Carpenter also murdered Le Van Minh."

She took the folded page, and gave a little soundless laugh. "It would be one for the law books, wouldn't it," she said, "getting an exhumation order on the evidence of a poem?" She said gently, "It's brilliant detective work, but it isn't likely to persuade a judge."

"Carpenter wasn't killed by accident, Tracy. That should weigh in the judge's mind. Along with Carpenter's suspicious actions on the dock the day they buried Mr. Le. And remember to take those bank statements I gave you."

"Oh, I will," she said doubtfully. "I wish to God Carpenter wasn't dead. All of this would be a lot easier."

"That's why he's dead," Dave said. "Has Flores found Don Pham? I hope bail was set at ten million dollars."

"Don Pham has vanished." She smiled thinly. "Not long ago, you told me Rafe Carpenter was no killer, remember?"

Dave made a sour face. "I was wrong. But I also told you it was time I retired." He got heavily to his feet. "And about that I was right. I'm bungling this case."

"Don't quit on me now," she said.

He went to the door. "They'll have to kill me first."

She paled under her freckles. "Not funny," she said.

14

He wasn't the only Westerner to choose the shiny, pastel-walled Hoang Pho, on its seedy waterfront street, as the place to eat lunch today. Hoang himself showed Dave a table. He did it as if he had lost the power of speech along with the ability to move the muscles of his face. He drew out a chair for Dave. Plainly Hoang would have been happier if Dave hadn't showed up ever again. Remembering Hoang's words about living with fear, Dave sat down, picked up a napkin, laid it in his lap, and took the menu Hoang offered him, still expressionless.

"Thank you," Dave said. Tables all around him were occupied. He lowered his voice. "And thank you for your help the other day. The results were interesting."

The little fat man murmured in his French accent. "I expected as much." He looked sober, "Though I disliked to put you into danger." He glanced watchfully around the room. "I have worried that perhaps harm came to you."

"A little excitement." Dave put on his reading glasses and glanced at the mysterious listings on the menu. "But no real harm. Not yet." He looked up into the man's moon face. "I worried for you. That Don Pham might come here." It was then Dave noticed the gray, bony, nondescript man in thick lenses. Where had he seen him before? He frowned to himself. It hadn't been long ago. Then he remembered Hoang, hovering at his elbow. "Everything all right with you?"

Hoang spread his hands. "As you see."

"Good." Dave closed the menu, handed it back. "I put myself in your hands." He pushed his reading glasses away. "I'll have whatever you suggest."

"And will you have a cocktail while you wait?"

Dave hadn't realized Hoang Pho's had a bar. He looked for it now and didn't see it. "A double martini, thanks," he said. "Straight up. Lamplighter. Twist of lemon."

With a quick bow, Hoang went away. He disappeared through swinging kitchen doors. No bar then, just a stock of booze in the refrigerator. Dave looked at the gray, thin man again. He sat in his gray suit and gray tie at a corner table, far from the windows, eating, and talking to a stocky Asian whose back was to Dave. The gray man seemed earnest, and was leaning forward to do his talking and listening. The Asian leaned forward too. They might have been television actors, told by a director to look conspiratorial.

Who the hell was the gray man? Dave knew it was just part of aging, so there was no point in fretting about it, but with everything else, his once sharp memory was developing leaks, and sometimes it made him frantic. Then it came to him. His second visit to the docks. The man had stood opposite Le Tran Hai in the doorway to the warehouse. Like Hai, he'd worn a hardhat, held a clipboard, and had checked items off a shipping manifest as forklifts jounced past, rolling crates into the looming building. Hai had been too busy to give Dave attention, too busy even for manners. He hadn't introduced the gray man. Dave judged him to be in his sixties, but this morning Hai had described Rafe Carpenter as "my most trusted and valuable employee." And Carpenter was only in his thirties. Yet the gray man had been doing an important job, teamed with the boss. While Carpenter was doing what—running the crane? Dave scowled.

He stopped scowling when the tiny young woman with the tinkling laugh brought his martini. He thanked her, tasted the drink. Icy perfection. He lit a cigarette and smiled contentment. The *pho*, when it arrived steaming in its bowl, kept him smiling. So did the savory little rolls of pork and God-knew-what in puff pastry. He was downing the last of these, when the gray man and the Asian got up from their table and headed for the door. The gray man glanced at Dave in passing, but there was no recognition in his eyes.

Then Dave wasn't noticing him anymore. He was noticing his stocky friend. His heart bumped. It was the man off the power launch, the one who had met Rafe Carpenter at the docks the day of Le Van Minh's funeral, and had walked off with the two attaché cases. Only distance had made it possible to mistake him for Don Pham. Though both stood about the same height and weighed about the same, the two men were wholly different. This man was flashy, with none of the gambling lord's quiet menace. This man moved with a self-satisfied swagger. This man smiled too much.

Hoang was trailing him, rubbing his hands, chattering, laughing. He opened the door to let them out onto the shabby, sun-struck street. Dave jerked bills from his wallet, laid them on the table, and followed, pushing the wallet away, taking long strides. Hoang caught his sleeve, frowning. "But, *m'sieur*, you have not finished your lunch."

"Who is that man?" Dave asked him.

"Chien Cao Nhu." The little restaurateur beamed after the swaggerer's departing back. "He is a dealer in sailing craft built in Taiwan. It is a splendid business for this area—brings many wealthy people here."

"Who may just stop in at the Hoang Pho to eat?"

Hoang nodded cheerfully. "He has only come here recently. From New York. We are all delighted. Plans are underway to honor him soon at a special banquet."

"Which you hope to cater, right?"

Hoang laughed. "Of course." Then he frowned. "*M'sieur* is troubled about something?"

"I don't think I'd count on that banquet."

Dave pulled the door open, half stepped out onto the sandy sidewalk. Chien Cao Nhu climbed into a glossy black Continental up the street. Not into the front. Into the back. A slim little youth in black opened the door for him. Turtleneck, tight jeans, leather jacket, he looked like one of Don Pham's doll-boys. Probably with a .357 Magnum strapped to his delicate ribcage. The Continental rolled off. The gray man got behind the wheel of a gray Honda, a late model but nothing pretentious. Dave turned back to Hoang. "Who's the man he lunched with?"

"I do not know," Hoang said. "It was before always another man. This man is a stranger to me."

Dave looked at him hard. "The other man—young, fair-haired, a dock worker?"

Hoang nodded. "Carpenter," he said. "Rafe Carpenter."

* * *

He followed the gray car. It wasn't a long drive. He hadn't expected it to be. The gray car slid down into the low-ceilinged cement fastness of parking levels where Dave had only a short time ago parked to visit Tracy Davis. The parking facility was under that bleak white square surrounded by new government buildings. Dave left the Jaguar not far from where the gray man left his Honda. He got into a red-doored elevator with the gray man, and watched him get off at the second floor. When the doors slid open to let him out, Dave saw on the opposite wall a big Federal seal. *U.S. Customs Service.* The doors closed.

He rode up another floor, took a down elevator to the second floor, got off. Under the Federal seal, facing steel-armed waiting-room chairs with fake leather cushions, a reception counter was flanked by ficus trees. Behind it, a tan-uniformed, middle-aged woman sat at a desk. He went and leaned on the counter. The woman was talking on a telephone. She gave him a smile, spoke for an another few seconds into the phone, then laid the receiver in place.

"What can I do for you?" she said cheerfully.

"You may think I'm not securely wrapped," Dave said, "but that man who just came in here, just got off the elevator at this floor? I'd swear he was an old friend of mine from high school. Ed Williams—right?"

"The thin man with glasses? Oh, no." She shook her head. "I'm sorry to disappoint you. That was Mr. Priest. Warren Priest. He's a chief Customs inspector."

"Priest? Are you sure?" Dave said. "Excuse me. Of course you are. But I could have sworn—"

She tilted her head at him, amused. "If you don't mind my saying so," she said, "weren't you and this Mr. Williams in high school rather a long time ago?"

Dave laughed. "Only a few decades. You're right, of

course. If we passed each other on the street, we'd neither of us know it, would we?"

"People do change." She smiled. "More's the pity."

Drycott Security Services had offices in a flat-roofed pale yellow structure up a side street of wholesale storage buildings—brick, dingy white paint, loading docks, rippled iron access doors, high wire fences, barred windows. A visitor to Drycott Security had to punch a button by a locked black wrought-iron gate. The bell push activated a surveillance camera over the front door of the place. The little click it gave in turning to focus on him, made him look up at it. It eyed him glassily. A voice came from a slotted black metal box next to the door, a cheerful young female voice.

"Thank you for coming to Drycott Security today. Please state your name and the purpose of your visit."

"My name is Brandstetter." Thankful it wasn't raining, he got out the ostrich-hide folder, opened it, held it up for the camera to look at. "I'm a private investigator, on assignment with the Public Defender's office of San Pedro County. I'm looking into the recent murder of Le Van Minh. He was your client—you guard the Le warehouse on the docks at the harbor. I have a couple of questions about that."

"Thank you, Mr. Brandstetter," said the cheerful voice. "I'll be back to you in just a moment." The sound clicked off. He lit a cigarette, turned, and watched a cat with kittens playing in a storage yard across the street. Something clanked behind him. He turned back. The voice said, "Thank you for waiting, Mr. Brandstetter. Please come in."

He dropped his cigarette, stepped into the narrow area between gate and front door, and the gate clanked behind him. When he put his hand on it, the door lock buzzed, he pushed the door, and was in a reception office that had no one in it to receive anybody—desk, chairs, a large painted plaster eagle on the wall, plants in corners, a standing U.S. flag. The door closed behind him, lock clicking quietly.

The cheerful young voice came out of a speaker over a door in the opposite wall. "Please go through the patio, sir. Mr. Drycott is expecting you."

The patio was sheltered by a sprawling, old avocado tree. Avocados large as softballs lay on the tiles. Dave's shoes rustled heaps of big dry leaves on his way to a bulky old man waiting for him in an open doorway. Drycott pumped his hand and laughed a hearty laugh that showed silver fillings in his back teeth—old G.I. dentistry.

"Brandstetter," he roared. "Proud to meet you. You're an ornament to our profession. You make us all look good." He slapped Dave on the back, and propelled him indoors. "Yes sir. I've seen you on television, read about you. Siddown." He waved a hairy paw at a visitor's chair. He dropped into a high-backed tufted leather executive chair back of a rangy desk. His face darkened. "Of course, I couldn't side with you against Colonel Zorn. The President didn't much like that either, but—the law of the land has got to be followed, I guess, even if it lets the Commies take over the world."

"Duke Summers put Zorn out of business," Dave said.

"Not I. You calling Duke Summers a Commie sympathizer?"

"Course not," Drycott said brusquely. "Never mind." He waved the memory aside. For the moment. When he'd walked in Dave had noticed beside a glass-fronted case of medals on Drycott's office wall, a photograph of Drycott with Ronald Reagan, Lothrop Zorn, and other military men. Among twenty photographs, mostly from

World War II, but some from later wars. Always wars. Drycott sat forward. "What can I do for you? These damn Vietnamese. Nothing but trouble. Downright subversive of those liberals in Congress to let them in, lend them money, teach them English. They're not like other people, Brandstetter. I know. I was sent over there by Jack Kennedy, in the first wave of advisers." He frowned and shook his head grimly. "Nothing's too low for the little yellow bastards. Never was. No morals at all."

"Le Van Minh was well thought of," Dave said.

Drycott grunted skeptically. "Not by somebody. Somebody murdered him. And probably with good reason."

"On the day of his funeral," Dave said, "I went down to the Le warehouse. Something funny was going on there, smuggling, I think—but I couldn't stop it. Your security guard ran me off. Only a skinny old man, but he had a gun."

Drycott's face twisted. "A skinny old man?"

Dave nodded. "At least seventy."

Drycott gave an amazed laugh, wagged his head, flicked one of many switches on a panel that blinked tiny lights. "Bring me the file on Le Electronics, please?"

"Yes, Mr. Drycott," a male voice said.

Drycott let go the switch, and blinked at Dave, head tilted. "You sure it was our logo on his shirt?"

"Drycott Security Services," Dave said.

"Reason I ask," Drycott said, "is that I never put anybody in one of my uniforms who's a day over forty. We don't hire pensioners. They can't protect anybody."

A straight-backed young man with a white sidewall haircut came in, laid a file folder in front of Drycott, turned with military precision, eyes front, and went straight out of the room again. Drycott opened the file, thumbed pages, peered at them. "Here it is. Day before the funeral, we got a call saying no guard would be needed that day. Place would be closed. Regular drive-by patrol would be enough."

"Let me guess who made that call," Dave said. "Rafe Carpenter, right?"

Drycott frowned, moving a finger on the page. "Right." He squinted at Dave. "Doesn't sound Vietnamese."

"No morals, though." Dave stood. "No morals at all."

15

He woke on the couch in the long back building and didn't know what time it was. The only light came from embers glowing in the iron basket in the fireplace. What had wakened him? Sounds from the bathroom. Numb, stiff in the joints, he shifted position, and a book tumbled to the floor. The frames of the reading glasses dug into his nose. He took them off, folded the bows. "That you?' he said.

"What?" Cecil was startled. He came and stood, a tall, lean silhouette between Dave and the hearth. "What are you doing down here?"

"Waiting for you," Dave mumbled. "What kept you?"

"Getting a feature together for tomorrow on the latest election polls. Never enough time."

"You could have phoned," Dave said.

"Ho. Look who's talking." Cecil switched on a lamp Dave remembered stretching a weary arm up to turn off just before his eyes had fallen shut. How long ago? He squinted at his watch. "Good Lord, it's two-thirty."

"And that," Cecil said, "is only because I hurried." He was back in the shadows jingling glass, ice, and bottles the bar. "I could hurry or I could phone. I chose to hurry."

"Never mind." Dave sat up, swung his feet to the floor. "You're here. That's all that matters." He moaned, yawned, rubbed a hand down over his face. "I wish Tracy Davis's lunatic half-brother had gotten into trouble someplace near here. The harbor's too far. All that driving wears me out."

Cecil came into the light and handed him Glenlivet over ice. Holding brandy in a small snifter, he sat on the raised hearth, saw the book on the floor, bent, and picked it up. "*The Vietnamization of America*. Man, can't you give it a rest?" Disgusted, he laid the book on the bricks. "Get your mind off it." He waved a long arm at the half-finished, half-stocked shelves. "Read a detective story."

"They don't fool me anymore." Dave drank some of his whisky. "No, I was looking for a reference to a certain Chien Cao Nhu."

"Oh, yeah? The one that used to broker sailing craft on Long Island Sound? Till somebody blew up his Mercedes? He wasn't in it, but the District Attorney set a Grand Jury to look into what happened, and Chien dropped out of sight."

Dave shook his head in wonder. "You are a fount of obscure information."

Cecil grinned. "I try to remember everything. They tell me it helps you get ahead in the news business."

"He's here now. Down at the harbor." Dave reached for cigarettes and lighter under the lamp. "Still selling sailboats from the enchanted Orient. And less attractive imports, I suspect." He lit a cigarette. "The Vietnamese community regards him as a prince of a fellow."

Cecil was watching him smoke. Grimly. "If you'd retire like you promised, you could quit cigarettes. It's the tension that makes you smoke."

Dave grunted. "Maybe you're right. Chien keeps interesting company." He told Cecil about his visit to Hoang Pho.

"They could have been talking boats," Cecil said.

"And I could be Mike Tyson," Dave said. "Warren Priest checks the shipments that come into the Le warehouse. Rafe Carpenter worked at the warehouse. Carpenter met Chien Cao Nhu at the warehouse when it was closed the day of old man Le's funeral. And gave him two attaché cases. Hai tells me no drugs or other contraband have ever been found by Customs in any Le shipment. What do you conclude?"

"They weren't talking boats?" Cecil said.

Dave laughed. "They weren't talking boats." He sobered. "Our friend Don Pham may have been right about the Le family. It's a beautiful house. But all that goes on there is not beautiful." Leaning back on the couch, he told Cecil about his morning there. "I understand the old woman perfectly, but I don't understand Thao, I don't understand Quynh, and for that matter, I don't understand Fergusson. They've got some kind of secret between the three of them, and I'm damned if I can figure out what it is."

"Ba's room—that must have been sad," Cecil said.

Dave nodded, drank some more of his whisky. "But the saddest place I saw today was Carpenter's."

Cecil looked startled. "You went there?"

"The American dream. Brand-new. Four bedrooms on a large lot of sloping green lawn overlooking the ocean. Pool, Jacuzzi, steam room—the works. Drug money is big money, no mistake. But what's going to happen now? The little kid wanders in and out. He understands his dad is dead. But he keeps looking for him. You can see that. His mother doesn't know where she is. Carpenter had her fooled completely. It took me an hour to get out of her that, yes, sometimes Rafe did go off on mysterious errands at night. More importantly, that he was home playing poker with three witnesses the night Le Van Minh was killed. I checked them all out. It's true."

"That wasn't what you went there to learn," Cecil said. "That sends you back to square one. Why did you go?"

"Looking for a skinny old man," Dave said. "The security guard who ran me off the docks that day."

"But why at Carpenter's house, of all places?"

"Because at Drycott Security Services, they didn't know him. Carpenter had rung and told them not to send a guard that day. Where would you look for him?"

"And was he there?"

"Not in person. Seems he's in Paris. Flew out the day after old man Le's funeral. But there was a framed photo of him on the piano. Holland Carpenter. Rafe's father." The telephone jangled. "Jesus." Dave sat up. "Now what?"

"I'll get it." Cecil set the snifter on the bricks and jogged to the desk. "Brandstetter's house," he told the receiver. "Who? What? Cotton? But he—all right. All right. Just be cool. We'll be there."

Frowning, Dave pushed up off the couch.

Cecil set down the receiver. "That was Lindy Willard. It's about Cotton."

"What about him?" Dave picked up his cigarettes and lighter. "He's supposed to be in New York."

"He's here, and she says he's been kidnapped."

"It doesn't make sense." Dave pushed the cigarettes and lighter into a jacket, shrugged into the jacket, and strode quickly through the shadows toward the door.

Cecil followed him. "Did you expect anything about Cotton Simes to make sense?"

"I sure as hell didn't expect him to come back." Dave felt in the jacket for keys. They were there. He pulled the door open. "He was scared to death when he got on that jet." He stepped out, waited for Cecil, closed the door, and they crossed the courtyard, headed for the Jaguar.

"Lucky we never take off our clothes," Cecil said.

"Do you really think so?" Dave said.

He had begun to dislike the harbor at night, the strong sea smell, the cold wind, coldest at this time, with sunrise an hour or so away. Nearing the Old Fleet, he had begun to look out for followers. Don Pham may have vanished, but Dave doubted he had given up. Cecil was doing the driving. At Dave's suggestion, he swung up extra streets, down alleys, doubled back. Twice they glimpsed a dark limousine—some undertaker looking for an address?—but they saw no black-clad little figures flitting into doorways.

They left the car on the street, by the crusty iron guard rails of the sea wall, and went down rickety steps to the unstable wooden walkways of the Old Fleet, where the shabby boats rocked asleep on black water. The scaly steel lampposts along the walkways were few and their bulbs gave only grudging light that reflected in yellow ripples below. Cecil pointed. Down the way, fairy lights twinkled in the rigging of the *Starlady*. Lindy Willard stood on top of the cabin, where she'd eaten croissants and drunk Bloody Marys with Dave the other morning. Clutching a mink coat tight around her, she peered anxiously in their direction.

"Now just a minute, there," a sharp voice said.

They stopped and peered into the darkness. A sturdy

little figure stood on the deck of the tubby boat. Bundled in a checked flannel bathrobe, a white sailor cap on her gray hair, the brim turned down. She cradled the orange and white cat on her left arm. Her right hand pointed a gun. A little copper-finish twenty-two pistol.

"Norma Potter," Dave said. "Where did you get that gun?"

"Ah, it's you, Mr. Brandstetter." She came towards them. "And who's that with you?" She gave a little shriek, and took a step backward. "Cotton?"

"Not Cotton," Cecil said, and gave his name. "I'm a friend of Mr. Brandstetter."

"You work for television news," she said. "That's right. You were down here before." She looked along the moorings. "Well, there's bad news tonight. Four of those little Asian boys in black were here. Two hours ago. They took Cotton away." She peered up at Dave. The cat slipped down, landed soundlessly on the deck, and scurried off. "I didn't even know he was still living here."

"Where did you get that gun?" Dave said.

"I didn't mean for you to see it," she said. "I found it on the deck here, the morning after Mr. Le was killed. I didn't know it was a twenty-two that killed him. Not then, not till you told me. Didn't look to me much better than a toy, but it might come in useful. Turned out I was right. After Andy was jailed, everybody around here just kind of gave up hope. So it's me for myself, isn't it? And I won't be sent packing, Mr. Brandstetter. I can't be. I've got no place to go. They have to let me stay here."

Dave reached for it. "Hand it over, please."

She clasped it to her breast with both plump hands. "I guess you don't know what 'desperate' means, do you?"

"There's no way you can shoot all the developers and bureaucrats and lawyers that want you people out. And if you could, you'd still have to move. To jail."

"I can always blow my brains out," she said.

"Don't do that," Dave said. "Who'd feed your cat?"

"You," she said promptly. "You're a fool for cats."

"Why didn't you shoot the doll-boys?" Dave said.

She passed the gun over to him, shamefaced. "Lost my nerve. I heard Cotton yell. I heard scuffling. And I got the gun from where I'd hid it and came up here swearing I'd shoot, but I couldn't make myself do it." She looked up at him again, her wrinkled face a pale small sad moon in the half darkness. "It takes a special kind of person to be able to kill somebody in cold blood, doesn't it?"

"A kind we'd be better off without," Dave said.

"Why didn't you call the police?" Cecil said.

"The phone's out there. In the dark." She waved an arm. "Old woman alone—I was afraid. Anyway, it was over, they had Cotton, they were gone. What could the police do?"

"They ought to know," Dave said. "I'll tell them."

Lindy Willard came down the metal ladder from atop the cabin faster than looked safe for a woman her age. In very high spike heels. Dave and Cecil had climbed on board. She came towards them with that regal sway of hers. She still wore the wig she'd performed in. Sequins glittered in it. But she had on jeans and a man's shirt under the fur coat. Gusts of Chanel Number Five came off the coat. Gusts of gin when she breathed at them. She glanced angrily back along the row of boats.

"What did old Norma want with you?"

"She saw the little boys in black take Cotton away."

"He was all right," she said in that glorious big voice that went echoing out across the water, "when I left at eight. He'd got here about six, buses, taxis."

"From the airport," Cecil said.

She nodded, turned. "Come inside." She led them into a teak-paneled cabin where purple velvet cushions were thrown around, framed gold and platinum records had been knocked off the walls, a table tipped over. "He must have fought back." She watched Cecil bend and right the table. "I never knew he had that kind of courage."

"What brought him back?" Dave said.

She stared, open mouthed. "You did," she said. "It's why I called you when I got home here after my last show, and he was gone. I figured you were the one to tell. What are you going to do about it?"

"Everything I can," Dave said. "But Cotton lied to you. I didn't send for him."

"Oh, my God." she began to shake. She moved to the far end of the cabin where bottles stood on shelves. She fumbled a glass, dropped it, got another, poured it half full of gin, the neck of the bottle rattling on the glass. She took a gulp from the glass and turned back to face Dave. "He said you instructed that public defender woman—what's her name?"

Dave felt cold in his belly. "Tracy Davis."

"She was the only one you said he could talk to here. Not me, not his sister, not you, nobody but Tracy Davis. And then only in an emergency, right? But there was no emergency. He didn't call her. She called him. She said he was to come back, you needed him, but he was more scared of phoning you, after you told him not to, scared it would get you killed."

Dave groaned. "Flores got to her, that son of a bitch. He wants Don Pham for the murders at the Hoang Pho, and Cotton's the only witness. I shouldn't have mentioned it to him last night. I'm getting senile."

"Somebody in the County building bugged their conversation, or taped into Tracy's phone call," Cecil said. "You said there's a leak there—that Don Pham always knows what the police are planning."

Dave watched Lindy work on the gin. "Then why didn't the doll-boys meet him at the airport?" He frowned. "For that matter, why didn't Flores meet him at the airport?"

"Because." She knelt and picked up a cigarette from among twenty that had fallen from a spilled silver box. She was wobbly, getting up. She sat on the coffee table and let Dave light the cigarette for her. "He took a plane two hours earlier than the one she said for him to take. Different airline too. He didn't trust her. Not really. Street smarts"—she smiled crookedly up at Dave through a haze of smoke—"are dumb smarts, but sometimes they pay off."

"For how long? Going direct to the first place they'd look for you is dumb," Cecil said. "If you'll forgive me."

"Nothing to forgive, child," she said wanly. "You are right." She waved a hand. "The evidence is before us." The gin was making her weepy. She wiped away a tear.

Dave frowned. "Why didn't Flores get here first?"

"Because Don Pham is always a jump ahead of him," Cecil said. "If he wasn't, he'd be in jail, wouldn't he?"

Dave grunted. "I'm beginning to wonder."

"Flores is probably lying awake in bed right now, trying to figure out why Cotton didn't get off the flight Tracy Davis told him to take, and walk into his waiting arms."

Lindy Willard said, "He would have jumped overboard and swum to China if he saw the police coming on board here for him. He came home because this Tracy Davis said it was you who wanted him. He wasn't going to her. No way. He was going to you. Tonight." Her head in the showbiz wig drooped and she began to cry in earnest. "He's dead, by now, poor, beautiful, sweet, funny boy. Lover. Lover."

"He's not dead." Dave patted her shoulder. "If they'd wanted him dead, they wouldn't have bothered to take him away. They'd have killed him right here."

She looked up quickly, hope in her eyes, mouth trembling in a try at a smile. "You think so? They won't kill him? Can you find him? Can you get Cotton back?"

"I can't find Don Pham," Dave said. "But he can find me. He's proved that before."

Cecil, picking up plaques, said, "No doubt about that."

Lindy's glass was empty. She tottered to her feet, and stumbled among cushions back to the bar. "Why would he?"

"Five o'clock in the morning," Dave said, "is not my brightest hour. When my mind starts working again, I'll think of something to bring him."

"Don't let it go too long," she said. "You know Cotton—that mouth of his. They could shoot him just to stop him jiving them." She laughed a woebegone little laugh. "More than a few times I could have done that myself."

"All right, all right," Raoul Flores said. "Back off, will you? I blew it. I'm sorry. You never make mistakes?" He was in bathrobe and pajamas in a clean, bright kitchen that smelled of chili peppers. Under wan electric light, he stood, beard stubbly, red-eyed, by a glistening stove, hoping water would boil in a red tea kettle so he could have coffee. He looked at his wrist where a watch should have been. He'd been rousted out of bed by Dave's pounding on his door in the first gray light of dawn, and had forgotten the watch. "Soon as the day shift comes on, I'll put out an APB."

"Put out search parties," Dave said, "with dogs. The meanest dogs you can find."

"I've got seventeen of those little poker-faced punks in cells waiting for a lineup so he can identify which two used Uzis on those men at the Hoang Pho that night, okay? I mean, I do my job, man—I do my job."

"Halfway," Dave said. "You should have rounded up Cotton first. What good is a lineup to a dead witness?"

"They wouldn't kill him," Flores grumbled.

"What else would they do?" Dave said. "But speaking of killing"—he took the twenty-two from his pocket and laid it on the kitchen table—"here's the gun that killed Le Van Minh."

Flores gaped. "Where the hell did you get that?"

"You didn't look very hard for it," Dave said, "or you'd have found it. Even little old ladies are too much for you."

"This is my house." Flores turned, face dark with anger. "Nobody talks to me that way in my house."

Dave slid back a door to a patio. "Fine. We'll talk outside. Your neighbors ought to hear this." He stepped out. The light was gray. Dew lay on metal lawn furniture in the patio. Spanish Dagger was a tall ghost in a corner of the wall. "You can't even protect secrecy in your offices. Don Pham knew Tracy had phoned Cotton as soon as you did."

Flores stayed by the stove. "You can't prove that."

"His boys snatching Cotton from the *Starlady* prove it."

"Hundreds of Asian kids dress that way," Flores said.

"And you managed to net seventeen—wonderful," Dave said. "What did you do, raid the corner noodle stand?"

"Who says the ones who took Simes were Don Pham's boys?"

"Maybe they weren't, but I don't think we're going to learn whose they were—not from you. Why isn't that lineup window dressing? Why did you really bring Cotton back?"

Flores's eyes narrowed. "To get the truth."

"For the citizens you serve—or for Don Pham?"

"Goddammit, you apologize for that."

"When you rescue Cotton." Dave pushed out through a plank gate in the patio wall. The hinges squeaked as the gate flapped shut. And in the kitchen, the kettle whistled.

16

Cecil kept nodding off, and Dave let him out at a taxi stand, so he could return to the canyon and get some sleep before he had to go to work. Dave had an appointment. He steered the Jaguar toward the docks. Twice he saw the dark limousine prowling the streets. Still trying to find the dear departed? He had his doubts. Early morning fog hung over the docks. A motorcycle stood chained to one of the uprights of the double-wire-mesh gates. He touched the machine. It was warm. A glance at his watch told him he was five minutes late, and he hurried down the zigzag staircase. The air was damp and cold. He ought to have brought his trenchcoat. Mist clung to his hands and face. Stacked crates kept him from seeing the door of the Le warehouse. When he stepped around the last stack, Herman Steinkrohn raised a hand to him. He wore a white crash helmet, boots, a brown leather jacket with a fur collar.

"What's this all about?" His boyish face was puzzled.

"Thanks for coming." Dave grinned briefly. "What it's about is how risky it is to say to me, 'If I can ever do anything for you, let me know.' It can cut into a man's sleep."

The blond kid laughed. "It's okay. I meant it." He frowned. "But what are we going to do?"

"We're going to find out what's in the latest shipments to Le Electronics from the Orient," Dave said. "Other than what's stenciled on the outside of the crates."

Steinkrohn squinted. "I don't get you."

"You know," Dave said, "that Rafe Carpenter was killed down here night before last?"

The boy looked grieved. "Yeah. They told us. We felt like going home, most of us. But you can't do that. Not without union approval. And it's a hassle to get that."

"You don't know why he was killed?"

Steinkrohn tilted his head. "He fell from the crane."

"Is that what Mr. Le told you?"

"Isn't it true?"

Dave told him what seemed to him to be true.

Steinkrohn whistled surprise. "Oh, wow. But Rafe? Are you sure? I mean, he was, like so—so—"

"Wholesome?" Dave said. "Straight arrow?"

"Yeah, right." Steinkrohn said this softly. But something bothered him. "Still, how could he be bringing drugs through here? The feds are here every time a shipment comes in. A dude called Priest. He's a main man at Customs."

"And he has a team of uniformed inspectors open every crate and go through it, top to bottom, does he?"

"Well, no—" Steinkrohn took off the crash helmet and ruffled his yellow hair. "Actually, they don't do anything. They play cards. No, Mr. Priest checks all the manifests, right along with Mr. Le."

"And that's it?" Dave said.

"That's all I ever saw him do," Steinkrohn said. His blue eyes showed confusion, then recognition. "It wasn't enough, was it?"

"What do you think?"

"I never thought about it before," Steinkrohn said. "It wasn't any of my business. My business—"

"I know. Your business was to load the crates onto a forklift truck and store them inside."

"You're saying Mr. Priest was in on the drug smuggling? Rafe paid him to only pretend to check the shipments?"

"After somebody else paid him."

"Who would they be?" Steinkrohn said.

"The ones who shot him," Dave said. "I don't know who they are. Not for sure. I'm trying to find out." He gave the kid a little smile. "You ready to get to work?"

"Sure." Steinkrohn nodded. "Only, how do we get in?"

Dave drew a packet of keys from his jacket pocket and tossed them to Steinkrohn. The boy caught them, peered at them. "These are Rafe's keys. I see him use them every morning." He stared at Dave. "Where did you get them?"

Dave didn't think Steinkrohn wanted to hear. Not really. "You know which one fits these locks?" he asked.

"Sure, but—" Steinkrohn didn't finish the thought. His eyes widened, he yelped, "Look out!" and somebody landed on Dave's back and bore him down to the deck. There was savage yelling. Dave glimpsed Steinkrohn wrestling with a kid about half his size, all in black, face masked. The creature on Dave's back was banging his shoulders and neck with karate chops. Dave twisted this way, that way. It did no good. He tensed, and heaved upward. The way a bronco dislodges a rider. It worked. He scrambled to his feet. The small black figure yelled and launched itself at him again. Dave spun out of the way. The boy staggered on past him. Steinkrohn had his little ambusher in both hands, raised him over his head, and with a roar like a grizzly bear's, threw him off the dock into the water. The other masked boy ran at him, screaming. Steinkrohn grinned, stepped aside, stuck out a foot, and the boy went head over heels, wailing, off the dock to join his friend.

Breathing hard, heart hammering, Dave leaned against the warehouse wall, and rubbed his neck and shoulders. Steinkrohn came to him. "You okay?"

"I'm too old for hand-to-hand combat," Dave gasped. "You did a nice job. You going to fish them out?"

"They're swimming away." Steinkrohn pointed across the water where freighters loomed in the fog. "Back to Vietnam, I hope. What did they want?"

Dave pushed away from the wall, and limped off.

"Where you going?"

"To check out a limousine," Dave said. "Come along, if you want to."

Steinkrohn walked beside him, the heels of his motorcycle boots clunking on the planks. "This is better than TV," he said. "I thought real detectives led dull lives."

"When they don't," Dave said, "they wish they did."

Steinkrohn looked into his face worriedly. "You don't sound like you feel too good."

Dave began to climb the steps up to the street. "I smoke too much, drink too much, eat too much rich food." He stopped, leaned against the rail to catch his breath. "In short, I abuse my health. It doesn't help when strangers join in." He pushed on. They reached the street.

"Jesus, there is a limousine. How did you know?"

"It's been following me for hours." Dave tried the door on the passenger side. It wasn't locked. The boys had been in a hurry to catch him. He bent and stretched bruised muscles, to reach into the glove compartment. He handed Steinkrohn a slip of paper.

"It's the mandatory insurance thing," Steinkrohn said. "I haven't got my glasses. What's the owner's name?"

"Le Huu Loi," Steinkrohn said.

"And do you by chance happen to know who that is?"

"Sure," the boy said. "Mr. Le's grandmother."

The fog had burned off. The sun was well up. Through the opaque wired glass of the warehouse windows, midmorning light slanted down on the dozens of clear plastic bags Dave and Steinkrohn had laid out on the tops of crates still not opened. They'd stopped after crow-barring the tops off five. Scores of new television sets, stereos, VCRs sat around in no order at all, shrouded in heavy plastic.

Dave had climbed to the catwalk and the office at the rear to make some telephone calls. And soon a crowd, police, Customs officers, Drug Enforcement agents, Coast Guard and Harbor Patrol officers, reporters, photographers, television sound and camera people, was milling around ankle-deep in packing materials, Excelsior, die-cut cardboard, and molded white Styrofoam on the concrete floor.

The transparent bags held white powder. Pure heroin. That was what the DEA and Customs officials called it— grim men in business suits. Warren Priest had been one of these, but not for long. Priest had soon gone off in handcuffs, and Raoul Flores had departed with men in blue uniforms to try to find Chien Cao Nhu. Armed DEA agents had followed. Dave watched them go with a wry feeling that Chien would not be at his fancy boatyard this morning, that Chien would be in that limbo which at the moment also concealed Don Pham, a place whose location somebody knew, but nobody dared name.

Dave looked down from the offices and, through the steel lattice work of structural supports, watched things grow calm and begin to get methodical on the floor below. The news crews left. Feds in neat jackets and slacks tagged the bags of heroin and loaded them into the trunks of unmarked cars parked outside the warehouse doors, where the glancing sun gave the vehicles a shine they didn't commonly enjoy. Uniformed Customs officers went to work prying open crates Dave and Steinkrohn hadn't got to. There were long aisles of them, stacked high. To probe them all would take days.

Except for the DEA, other law enforcement personnel slowly cleared out. It seemed to Dave as if he had talked to every one of them. As for the news people, after answering the questions of the eighth television reporter, half blinded from still photographer's strobelights, he'd fled up here—and found Le Tran Hai seated at his desk, stunned, motionless. He had answered a thousand questions, had laid all his records in the hands of DEA agents, had sent his warehousemen and office staff home with instructions to stand ready for questioning. What was left? Dave sat down across from him. Hai's dull eyes gradually focused. He asked hoarsely:

"What is my grandmother's car doing here?"

"She wanted to stop me having Le Doan Ba's body exhumed for an autopsy. It looks as if she lent the car to a pair of street punks and paid them to beat me up. They followed me all night. Luckily they didn't jump me until Steinkrohn was here to act as my bodyguard."

Hai said something in Vietnamese that sounded like a curse. In English, he said in a broken voice, "We are disgraced. We are destroyed. My poor father."

"I'm not going to bring charges against your grand-mother," Dave said. "And no one believes you knew about Carpenter's drug smuggling. You're not destroyed. Forget that. It's a thriving business. The DEA will clear you, this trouble will pass and be forgotten."

Hai heavily shook his head. "I was not alert. It was my responsibility to see that the laws were strictly obeyed by this company in all its dealings." He looked bleak. "I cannot live with such dishonor." He made a strange, stiff gesture to indicate what had happened out there in the warehouse. "To allow a hateful poison to enter this country which had been so generous to us—" He struck his forehead with the heel of a hand. "How stupid I was."

"It was Rafe Carpenter who committed the crime," Dave said. "It was Rafe Carpenter who was stupid, and venal, and a good many other sad things. Not you. He betrayed you."

Hai jumped out of his chair. "I have no excuse. I am not blind. I ought to have seen." He turned his back, and pummeled his head with his fists. "I was a fool to trust him. The gods have spoken plainly. My young brother dies. My father is killed. This business is corrupted. All because of my stupidity." He faced Dave, tears running down his face. "From this day, the whole world will sneer when the name of Le is spoken."

He yanked open a desk drawer, scrabbled in it, brought out a knife. The blade flashed in the window light. Dave threw himself across the desk, gave a wide, painful swing of his left arm, struck Hai's wrist, and the knife went flying. "No—I must die, I must die." Hai dropped to the carpeted floor, groping for the knife, and Dave was down there shouldering him away, grabbing the knife, struggling to his feet. He said, "You can't kill yourself. Who'll look after the business, the family, your wife and children?"

Hai sat on the floor, rumpled, sobbing. Dave stuck the knife into his waistband, bent and helped Hai to his feet. There seemed no strength left in the man. Dave got him into his chair. "I'll get you some water." A cooler waited in the outer office where the computer screens stood in rows mute and gray as gravestones. He took a paper cup of water back to Hai, who accepted it blankly, drank it, sat staring at nothing, cup in his hand. Dave's heart labored. He was short of breath. "I'll tell you one thing," he said. "It may make you feel a little better. It wasn't Rafe Carpenter who killed your father."

Hai's head jerked up. "It wasn't?"

"He was playing cards that night, and the men with him all say he never left the game. Neighbors. I checked with all of them. An avocado grower, and two businessmen—hardware, mixed concrete—none of them connected to shipping, importing, anything like it. They only knew Carpenter slightly. No reason I could find for them to lie for him."

"Then who did kill my father?" Hai said.

A DEA officer appeared in the doorway, a pink-skinned young man, going bald. Roche—was that his name? "We don't need to keep you any longer today, Mr. Le. We'll be sealing the warehouse, and we'll advise you when we've finished our work here. I think you supplied us with all the data we'll need. If not, we'll be in touch. Everything will have to be thoroughly vetted. We'll need to interview all your employees, so I'm afraid it's going to take a few days."

"No problem." Le Tran Hai spoke the words dully. He pushed up out of his chair. "I will, of course, cooperate in every way." He tried to work up a smile and failed.

"Thank you." Roche came inside to shake Dave's hand. "And Mr. Brandstetter—thank you, sir. You're as good as your reputation."

Dave smiled. "What are you talking about?"

"We worked with Warren Priest for years and never caught him. It only took you one day."

"He got careless," Dave said, "and I got lucky."

The loft smelled of sunlight and pine sap. Cecil sat up naked in the broad bed under the open skylight, knees clutched in his arms, and glowered, watching Dave shed his jacket, tie, and shirt. "You cut me out of the biggest story of the month." Dave was desperate for sleep. He wasn't up to hours like the ones he'd just kept, not anymore. He felt bruised in every part of his being. A hot shower would help, but he hadn't the strength left for it. He sat on the bed's edge and gave a groan. Cecil said, "You knew what you were going to find, and you didn't tell me."

"I apologize," Dave said, prying off shoes, peeling off socks. "I didn't think."

"Don't give me that. You never stop thinking."

"Okay. That limousine bothered me, all right? I had a hunch about it." He unbuckled his belt, unlatched the waist band, ran down the zipper, and hiked his butt to get his trousers off. "I couldn't shake the idea that I'd seen it before. And of course, I had. At Mr Le's funeral." He folded the trousers indifferently, and tossed them at a chair. They slipped off the chair to the floor, and he didn't care. "I wondered if I'd been wrong about Hai—that maybe he was after me. But whoever it was"—Dave tossed away his briefs, lay back on the bed with a sigh, and shut his eyes—"I didn't want you hurt, okay? You've been hurt often enough, because of me." He yawned.

"Getting that story wouldn't have hurt," Cecil grumbled. "It would have helped. Who was in the limousine?"

Dave told him, trying to keep from drifting to sleep.

"You didn't care if Steinkrohn got hurt?"

"He handled it like an everyday occurence."

"You're lucky he was there waiting for you."

Dave turned on his side. "You didn't miss the story. The story isn't over yet." He groped out for Cecil. "Come on. Curl your fine brown frame against my back."

"'Fine Brown Frame' is a Nelly Lutcher number," Cecil said. "Lindy Willard never sang that one." But he did as Dave asked. And Dave smiled contentment. Cecil said, "What do you mean, the story isn't over? Rafe Carpenter's father set up the deals at the Far East end, and Rafe took care of the shipments once they arrived. Isn't that how it was? And the not so priestly Mr. Priest covered for them for a price. And Chien Cao Nhu was the buyer here. What more is there?"

"Who killed Le Van Minh?" Dave said.

"Why wasn't it Andy Flanagan after all?" Cecil said. "With that little gun he tossed on Norma Potter's boat?"

"Because Don Pham doesn't think so," Dave murmured. "I haven't found the killer for him, yet. When I do, he'll pay us another visit."

"I can hardly wait," Cecil said.

Dave laughed and fell asleep.

17

Sleekly groomed, Le Thi Nga was as commanding as she'd looked coming down the church steps behind the coffin at her husband's funeral, a woman in control, not just of a chain of successful restaurants and the staffs who ran them for her, but of herself. She had heard Dave's name and read his license, undismayed. Why? Surely Hai had told his mother of the calamity at the warehouse, and that Dave had triggered it. Yet she'd calmly ordered a bottle of white wine and a plate of fresh, spicy little shrimp appetizers, and sat with him in a quiet booth of Madame Le's Pearl of Saigon restaurant, only an hour before the lunchtime rush, relaxed, attentive, wearing a polite and patient smile.

She was as unlike her son-in-law, the nervous, harried Matt Fergusson, sweating and stammering through his interview with Dave here the other night as could be. And Dave remembered fat and frightened little Hoang Duc Nghi, in his shiny eatery down at the waterfront—

with his speech about going to sleep in fear, waking up in fear, learning to live with it. Surely Le Thi Nga had gone through the same harrowing times, experienced the same losses, the same narrow escapes. Beyond those, she'd just had a husband shot to death, and had buried a grown son. Yet, sipping her wine, nibbling on the small edibles, she seemed almost serene. He wondered how she did it.

"Was it the truth Quynh told me?"

Listening to his story, his questions, she had looked unwaveringly into his eyes. Now she looked away. "My children were taught from the beginning always to be truthful."

"But we don't remain children," Dave said. "Life puts strains on what our parents taught us was right and wrong. Sometimes those strains are too great."

She picked up the dewy green bottle and refilled Dave's glass. "You have lived long," she said with a smile, "and you speak wisely."

"I think she loves her husband very much," Dave said.

A wry smile twitched Madame Le's perfect mouth. "Very much," she agreed. "Enough so that she dared to argue with her father, who did not want her to marry an American."

"He didn't like Matt Fergusson?"

"Liking," she said, "was not the question. He felt it a breach of tradition. He wanted Quynh to marry someone from her own culture and background." She gave Dave a quick grim glance and looked away again. "Children of mixed race have a terrible life in Vietnam."

"And here?" Dave said. "They look well and happy."

"My husband did not believe that would be so," she said, "and he was stubborn, but Quynh's love was stronger than his angry denials. In the end, she won his permission."

"And you?" Dave wondered. "How did you feel about it?"

"I was the one who introduced Matt to the family," she said. "I found him working at a place called Al Fresco in West Los Angeles, and I saw at once that he was exceptional. My little enterprise"—the wry smile came again—"had grown from one tiny café to two and three and four, and I was desperate for someone to take on half of the duties, someone young, intelligent, energetic. Matt was all of these things, and he had no prejudices against Vietnamese people. He loved our ways, our culture, he understood with his heart."

"And he and Quynh fell in love. Would she lie for him?"

Madame Le opened her eyes wide and laughed. "Ah, you are not to be deflected from your purpose, I see."

"Nguyen Hoa Thao was there that morning," Dave said, "and Quynh looked at her. I thought there was some special meaning in that look. And she asked Thao if it wasn't true that she, Quynh, had been here at this restaurant with Matt the night Le Van Minh was murdered. And after a pause, Thao said to me that it was true. It didn't convince me."

She frowned. "And you wish me to say—?"

"Wasn't Quynh right there at your house when Andy Flanagan telephoned your husband to come to the docks that night?"

Madame Le drank some of her wine. She picked up and set down again another of the little appetizers. She studied him, drew a breath, and asked, "If I were to tell you that, yes, she was at home, what would this mean to you?"

Dave was lighting a cigarette. He looked at her across the flame. "What would it mean to you?"

"That since you never believed Andy Flanagan killed

my husband, and it now seems out of the question that Rafe Carpenter did so, you have decided Matt must have done it."

"Deciding is for judges and juries." Dave drank wine and gently smiled. "But I do wonder where he was that night. Had something gone wrong between him and Mr. Le?"

She blanched, jerked, knocked over her glass. Wine splashed her dress. She wiped at it with a napkin. Was she angry or afraid? Whichever, her composure was gone. "Of course not. What a thing to suggest."

"I didn't suggest." Dave said mildly. "I only asked a question. I think Quynh and Thao and Matt share a secret. Something between them they don't want anyone to know. What would that be? Can you guess?"

She stood. "Haven't you harmed the Le family enough? Claiming that Ba was murdered. Digging up his poor little body. Ruining my husband's business, of which he was so proud. Humiliating my wonderful son Hai."

"That was Rafe Carpenter's doing," Dave said.

"Leave us alone, Mr. Brandstetter. Have we no right to our secrets? Who says you should know them?"

"Murder," Dave said. "Murder says so."

After learning from a waiter at Al Fresco what he had expected to learn, Dave hung up the gritty receiver of the shopping center pay phone and turned away gloomily. Noon sun blazed down on the vast spread of glassy storefronts, the rows and rows of parked cars. Angrily he wished it all gone, wished the brown hills open as they'd been fifty years ago when he was young. Wished the white-faced cattle back on the oak-shadowed hills, wished for the drowsy green of endless orange groves along narrow, dusty roads. Not mile after mile of tract houses beside eight-lane freeways.

Moodily he flapped out of his jacket as he trudged to the Jaguar. When he opened its door, heat poured out. He tossed the jacket inside, switched on the engine so the air conditioner would blow out the oven air. Standing beside the car, waiting for this to happen, he was glum. The aim of his work had never changed, to get at the truth no matter who got hurt. That would maintain, if he kept at it into the next century. But he wouldn't. He hadn't the stomach for it anymore. Let somebody else do the wrecking after this—of lives, of hopes, of fortunes. The wrong-doers he didn't give a damn for. It was the blameless ones.

He got into the car where the air was cool now, slammed the door, drove out of the vast parking lot onto a wide white concrete boulevard streaming with traffic. Miles to the east, he found a quiet hilly enclave of new condominiums and town houses on winding streets, with handsome lawns and plantings. The place where Sam Dupree lived faced the photogenic rolling green acres, ponds, tree clumps of a golf course. Dave pushed a bell button, chimes sounded on the other side of a carved front door, and he tried to think of a replacement for the tired phrase "with a heavy heart." Nothing came to him.

The boyish man of fifty who opened the door wore a trendy unbleached muslin shirt and jeans and was barefoot, but he still managed to look dapper. He peered at Dave uncertainly. He looked past Dave, seeming to think somebody he knew might be with him. Or should be. Wariness was in his tone that rose on the one simple syllable. "Yes?"

"Sam?" Dave smiled and held out a hand. "Dave Brandstetter. We met at Whit Miller's in Malibu. His annual New Year's bash. Remember? When was it? Nineteen eighty-one?"

"Ah, yes, of course." Dupree had a ready smile. A little too ready, a little too eager to please. You ran into this with young, scared homosexuals—or used to once upon a time. The way a dog wags its tail, they turned on the smile, the charm, desperate for acceptance, forgiveness, attention, love, table scraps, bones, anything, but just don't kick me. What he saw in Dupree's manner was a snatch of badly faded film. Dupree shook Dave's hand. "How are you? You look splendid. What brings you out this way?"

"A case I'm working on," Dave said.

"Oh? Sandy Fine told me you'd retired." He said it accusingly, annoyed at having believed the wrong gossip. "What sort of case?"

"The usual," Dave said. "Murder."

"Just like TV." Dupree clapped his hands. "Jessica Fletcher in drag." Again he peered past Dave's shoulder. "Are the cameras rolling?" He patted his hair—not a gray strand in it. "May I run back to makeup? Is there time?"

Hadn't he just come from there? No middle-aged man's skin was naturally that smooth. Dave said, "May I come in?"

"Am I a suspect?" Dupree shivered with delight.

Dave said, "Matt Fergusson is a suspect."

Dupree stopped smiling and looked his age. "Oh, God," he whispered. He backed into a hallway. "Yes, yes. Come in, come in." Dave stepped past him, Dupree closed the door and walked away quickly. Dave followed him into a living room of white French furniture, scattered newspapers, a half-empty coffee cup. A wide window overlooked the golf course. Dupree set a tiny motor singing that closed the curtains. Before the light was gone, Dave saw and picked up from a coffee table a padded leather photo album. Dupree turned, stared blankly at Dave, said, "What are we doing in here? Come to the kitchen." The kitchen was built around a center burner deck. Lots of cupboard space. Hanging pots. Hanging bunches of herbs and peppers. Cutting boards. Three ovens. Dupree stood in the midst of it, hands raised, unable to think what to do. At last he said, "Yes, of course. A drink."

Dave laid the photo album on a counter and turned its pages. They held photograph after photograph of Sam Dupree with young, blond, blue-eyed, good-looking Matt Fergusson—at the beach, in mountain snow, on cruise ships, in a gondola on a canal in Venice, on camels in Egypt, the long ends of striped turbans blowing. The photos were dated in ballpoint. The trips had ended six years ago. After that the photos were mostly of Fergusson solo. On a diving board at an apartment complex pool. Eating at a patio table set for two. Sometimes the photographer's shadow showed. It was always Dupree's shadow. Dave turned another page. He got a glimpse of Fergusson naked lying on a rug asleep in front of a fireplace, of Fergusson naked, grinning seductively from a rumpled bed. A hand came and firmly closed the album.

"It didn't stop when he got married," Dave said.

"He insisted it had to." Dupree stroked the album cover wistfully. "I was desolated, but I know when I'm beaten, and I agreed." A rueful smile twitched his mouth. "I made the best of it, tried to forget him. Kept myself busy remodeling Al Fresco, improving the menu."

"It's a nice place," Dave said. "I eat there sometimes. For the *pêche chocolat flambé*. I didn't know it was yours, or I'd have looked you up and said hello."

"I'm sorry you didn't." Dupree spoke absentmindedly, but now he seemed able to act. He found glasses and ice cubes, tomato juice, lemon peel, Worcestershire sauce and vodka, and put the drinks together while he talked. "I even wrote that cookbook I'd been threatening to for years. Just what the world needed. One more cookbook. But I had cartons positively gravid with recipes. Sorting them and deciding which to use and which to throw away kept me occupied. When I wasn't occupied, I tended to weep." He came and put a glass into Dave's hands. He smoothed the pouches under his eyes. "And you know what that does to one's beauty."

"Right." Dave tasted the Bloody Mary. It had an uncommon lot of vodka in it. He gave a soft whistle and lifted the glass to Dupree. *"Un bebida fuerte."*

"I hate a wishy-washy drink," Dupree said.

Dave said, "So you respected the marriage, but Fergusson couldn't cut it, and he came back, and the two of you took up your relationship as before."

"Well, hardly. I mean, the Ming empress of a mother-in-law keeps him working day and night. If he gets over here once a week, it's a miracle from God, and you know how stingy She is with those." Dupree drank from his glass and grew solemn. "It's Mr. Le's murder you're investigating, right?"

"Has Fergusson talked to you about it?"

"He was absolutely devastated," Dupree said.

"Why? It was Madame Le who gave him his break."

"It wasn't that. It was that Mr. Le was always kind to him, and the night he was killed, there'd been a terrible row at dinner, and Matt had screamed at him that he was a heartless old tyrant and other cordialities of that sort. And now, of course, he was wracked with guilt."

Dave frowned. "What was the argument about?"

"The marriage. I mean"—Dupree waved a hand in a

gesture of hopeless incomprehension—"it happened six years ago. There are two lovely children. Little dolls."

"You've met them?" Dave said.

"Surprises you, doesn't it? But Matt loves me, and he loves Quynh, and he loves those children, and nothing would do but we must all become friends." Dupree made an unhappy face. "I hate that, but to keep the peace, I had them all here one Sunday. Of course, they have no idea what Matt and I are to each other. I was an ex-employer. An old friend."

"Yup," Dave said. "The row at the dinner table?"

Dupree sighed and shrugged. "I never got the straight of it. Originally, Mr. Le had fought against Quynh marrying Matt, all that awful old nonsense about mixing the races and so on." Dupree gulped from his glass, wiped tomato juice off his lip. "But he'd given in, and he'd been sweet and generous to Matt and Quynh, and he'd doted on the grandchildren. And now, suddenly, he was demanding an end to the marriage."

Dave frowned. "For what reason?"

Dupree shook his head. "Business? A debt owed to some old friend? Matt never finished telling me. He was too upset. His father-in-law was dead, and Matt had been ugly to him that night. He wanted to beg the man's forgiveness. And it was too late." Dupree blinked back tears. "It was heart-rending to watch him, poor child. He was really in agony."

"Surely you exaggerate," Dave said.

"I don't," Dupree said crossly. "Not this time."

"You didn't think his agony might be about something more serious than a few words spoken in anger?"

Dupree looked puzzled. "What are you saying? That Matt—oh, no, you're wrong. Matt is not a suspect."

"He claims he was at the Pearl of Saigon, working on the books, the night Mr. Le was killed. But he can't prove it. He was angry at the man. Why didn't he kill him?"

"We're talking about the night of the eleventh, right?" Dupree said. "Well, forget it. He was here with me, and I *can* prove it because, with her usual exquisite sense of timing, my dear mother was also here. Torture. Matt and I get so little chance. And she didn't leave till midnight." He grimaced. "Probably for an urgent meeting of her coven."

Le Huu Loi lay in bed in a room where the blinds were closed. The carved elevated bedstead was large, and made her look tinier than ever. Her gray hair, elaborately put up with combs when he'd met her, lay spread on the pillow. Colors were muted in the darkened place, but he gauged the carved screens near the bed would glisten with nacre and cinnabar in sunlight, and that the carpet underfoot was rich with crimsons and blues. Quynh had ushered Dave into the room, and while he stood at the foot of the bed, she stood beside the old woman and held her bony hand. The rasp of the old woman's voice had become today a whispering together of the brown, dry leaves of bamboo. Her eyes glittered, sunk in their sockets. She watched Dave, but she spoke Vietnamese again, and Quynh translated.

"She asks your forgiveness," Quynh said, without turning her flower face in Dave's direction. "It was wrong of her to have you assaulted as she did. You are an official. She respects the government of the United States, and loves this country." Quynh listened again for a moment. "She is most grateful that you do not intend to prosecute her."

"Tell her it's all right, that I understand her reasons. Officials here don't always deserve respect, but the exhumation of Ba's body was necessary. Before coming here today, I spoke by telephone to the County medical examiner. He says that Ba was suffocated, as I thought. Someone took Ba's life. It was no accident."

Quynh nodded. "The medical examiner telephoned this information to our doctor, and he came here with the news. She was up and about and vigorous before his visit. Now she is . . . as you see."

"Then tell her I am sorry for the loss of her grandson in this terrible way, and that I believe he was a fine poet, whose work she can take pride in." He looked at the old woman and said, "I hope you will feel strong and well again soon. Thank you for your apology."

The old woman probably understood him, but Quynh translated anyway, and the old woman answered in Vietnamese, looking at him. She ended her words by opening and closing her eyes, and he bowed, turned, pushed curtains aside, and walked out into the sunlit courtyard. He heard Quynh's voice murmuring for a moment in the shadowed room. Then she came out, and rolled the door shut behind her.

"How is Le Tran Hai today?" Dave asked her.

"He is meeting with our father's attorneys." She stood at the edge of the pool, watching the big, slow golden carp loaf in the shadows of the lily pads. "He believes he will be prosecuted and sent to prison." She looked at Dave. "He thinks no one will accept that he knew nothing about it."

"What do you think?" Dave said. "He's your brother. You've known him all your life."

"Hai is good and kind and honest, but sees only what is obvious." Her smile was solemn. "He never understood what was not strictly—regular. He has no sense of humor or of play or of imagination. He was solemn even as a small boy, and always corrected me and Ba for the smallest childish misdoings. He was as stern with us as

our father. More so. I am sure he knew nothing of what
Rafe Carpenter was doing. He would read of such crimes
in the newspapers, or see them on the television, of
course, and, like father, he would be outraged and
disgusted. Particularly if Vietnamese were involved. But
that drug smuggling could be taking place under his very
nose"—she shook her head sadly—"would simply never
cross his mind. No, I must believe he knew nothing of it.
But he is frightened, Mr. Brandstetter. And ashamed,
since he ought to have known. It was his responsibility."

"I've told him not to worry," Dave said. "And you tell
him that if his lawyers don't think they can clear him, I
have one I'm pretty sure can." He took out his wallet,
slid a card from it, put the card into her hand. "He can
call me any time." Pushing the wallet away, he glanced at
the house. "Where's Thao, today?"

Quynh blinked surprise at him. "Why, she has left.
Only this morning. She had her own car, you know. A
rental car." She glanced at a small watch on a small wrist.
"Just an hour ago. For the airport, to fly home. To Paris.
Her visa expires today." Quynh frowned. "Is something
wrong?"

"You tell me," Dave said. "Why had she come here?"
Quynh's face became a mask. Dave waved a hand. "No,
please don't recite that nonsense about a courtesy visit as
ambassador from her father to yours. She had a mission."

"I don't know what you're talking about," Quynh said.

"I'm talking about the subject of a fierce argument at
the dinner table in there"—he gestured at the silent
sunlit walls of the house—"the night Le Van Minh was
murdered. An argument about your marriage."

She paled. "How could you know about that?"

"Matt told a friend, and that friend told me," Dave
said. "Your father demanded that you go to Nevada and
divorce Matt—isn't that so?"

She looked every way but at him. "You must not ask these things. This was a family matter."

Dave looked at his own watch. "Let's not waste time. Someone murdered your father, and it wasn't Andy Flanagan, and it wasn't Don Pham, and it wasn't Rafe Carpenter—"

"So you think it was Matt Fergusson," she said. "It's him you're after, now, isn't it? Well, I told you. He was at Madame Le's Pearl of Saigon that night. I know. I was there with him."

"The restaurant was closed and locked. No one was there. You lied about that, and got Thao to back your lie."

"Well, he didn't kill my father," she said. "He couldn't do such a thing. He isn't that kind of man."

"But the day I asked you, you were afraid he might have done it, weren't you? That was why you lied. You knew he was very angry with your father."

She shook her head desperately. "They were the best of friends. He worshipped my father."

"Until your father ordered you two to separate so Matt could marry Thao and make her an American citizen."

"What?" She laughed in derision. But the laugh was hollow. "That's ridiculous."

"Not to Thao's father. He couldn't come to the United States. The government wouldn't allow it. And he wanted to do business here. Not public business, private business, so there was just one person he could trust as his agent in the U.S. He'd have sent a son, but his sons were dead in the war. So he had to send Thao. It would take years for her to become an American citizen, but only six weeks in Reno for you to divorce Matt. Mr. Nguyen knew Mr. Le would do as he asked. Under the cold codes of correct behavior, he had no choice. Nguyen believed Thao would obey him, he believed you would obey Mr. Le."

"Business?" She mocked the word. But shrilly. "What sort of business could Thao manage? She's only a child."

"He was an old friend of the Le family. You tell me what sort of business."

"He was a politician," she said, "not a businessman."

"But a politician in exile is out of a job," Dave said. "He was a wealthy man, I understand. Able to fund your father, who was left penniless when he had to flee Vietnam. Maybe the money Mr. Nguyen is supposed to have embezzled from the U.S. in Saigon is running out. Maybe he has to get into business to maintain his life style."

"I know nothing of Mr. Nguyen's affairs," she said.

"Neither do I, but I know that Rafe Carpenter's father flew off to Paris the day after your father's funeral. And we both know the business Carpenter was in."

Quynh gaped. "You mean drug smuggling?"

"Drugs bring big money," Dave said, "and the area of the world where Mr. Nguyen used to wield power supplies a lot of drugs." He read his watch again. "Now tell me I'm right—your father was demanding you divorce, wasn't he, and Thao's time was running out, and Mr. Le wasn't having any more. He wanted obedience, and he wanted it then and there. And Matt cursed him and stormed out, didn't he?"

She hung her head. "Yes," she murmured.

"And I gather that when Andy Flanagan rang the telephone here shortly after ten that night, the whole house was still in turmoil. Your mother-in-law says you were here, and I know where Matt was—"

"Where?" she said.

"With Sam Dupree," Dave said. "Hai was here. He argued with your father, didn't want him to go to the Old

Fleet. Not alone. But your father was stubborn. He got six thousand dollars in cash he kept in the house—"

"In a safe in his bedroom," she said.

"And he drove off into the night. Did Hai follow him?"

"He tried. He stood in front of the gate to keep Father from opening it, and Father pushed him aside. He was still shouting at Hai as he went to get into the car. Hai tried to prevent him, but Father ordered him back, and Hai had no choice. He would never go against what our father wished."

"And where were you at that time, and your children, and where were Madame Le, Hai's wife, his children?"

"In the courtyard. Madame Le was present. Hai's wife and children had come out to see what the uproar was about, but she had sent them back to their rooms. My children are small, as you know, and they were asleep in their beds."

"And Thao? Asleep in her bed, too, right?"

"Didn't I tell you she was a child?" Quynh said.

"You did, but you were wrong." Dave headed for the red house door. "I need to use your telephone, please."

18

"**W**ell, that finishes that."
Raoul Flores ran a hand down over his sweaty terra cotta
face. His shirt collar was loosened, the knot of his tie
dragged down. He looked rumpled. It was the end of a
long day. He walked wearily back to his desk, and
dropped into the chair there. Desk and chair were in an
office not much different from that of Tracy Davis, in the
same building as Tracy Davis's. Tracy was present too.
She stood in a corner where a file cabinet had a jar of
flowers perched on top of it, keeping as far from Dave as
she could get without leaving. She watched him through
her green-rimmed spectacles, showing hurt feelings.
When he'd arrived at the county building ten minutes
ago, he'd stopped in to bring her with him from her
office. But without words. He was angry at her about
Cotton.

Flores said, "Thao bought the gun." He picked up the
permit issued to Nguyen Hoa Thao, and mailed to the
hardware store where she'd paid for it and where they'd

189

held it for her until the license came. He waved it at Dave, and dropped it in disgust back onto the desk top. "It was the gun that shot old man Le, all right. No mistake about that. She only bought it for one reason— and that was it. Her old man shipped her off to the States with orders to marry Matt Fergusson—and she was in love with some French kid, some student at the Sorbonne or something, and she did not care how many fathers ordered her to do different, she was not about to give in to them."

Tracy looked at Dave. "How did you find the gun?"

Dave told her.

Flores said, "My bet is Norma Potter thought Andy Flanagan killed Le. And hiding his gun would make it hard for us to prove it. She didn't want him convicted. Not that she liked him, nobody likes him"—he threw a sour glance Tracy Davis's way—"well, almost nobody— but it would put the Old Fleet protestors in a bad light."

"You can ask her." Dave nursed a paper cup of cold coffee and tilted back his chair. "But I doubt she'll tell you. Anyway, you're processing Flanagan out, are you?"

Flores shrugged. "No way to tie him to the weapon. Kenny, Le Tran Hai's teen-aged son, knew Thao had the gun." Flores smiled faintly. "Had a crush on her, used to go to her room when she wasn't around and paw through the drawers of her dresser, touching her things. She wore quite a perfume, did little Miss Thao."

Tracy wrinkled her nose. "It's still in this room."

"And he found the gun there?" Dave said.

"It got to be routine with him, taking it out and handling it," Flores said. "Sometimes he thought he'd kill himself with it. There in her room, on her bed." Flores chuckled ruefully and shook his head. "Fifteen-years-old. She wouldn't even look at him, and he was dying of love for her." Flores blew out air and nodded.

"Yeah. It was always there in the same drawer. Until the day after Le Van Minh was killed. Then Kenny couldn't find it anywhere."

"The others didn't know?" Dave asked. "Quynh and Matt?"

Flores shook his head. "It wasn't a conspiracy. Hell, she bought it when she was only two days off the plane from Paris. She knew all along old Le wouldn't give in."

"She had doubts," Dave said. "Or she'd have killed him sooner. When I talked to her, she was aching to get home to that French boy. She hung back until the last moment, hoping Le would relent. There surely would have been easier opportunities to kill him, living right there in the house with him, night and day." Dave lit a cigarette and blinked at Flores through the smoke. "How did she manage it? How was it Don Pham's boys didn't see her?"

Flores shrugged. "It is not exactly Disneyland's Parade of Lights out there. It was dark, there was no one around, but even if there had been, she was so angry she says she would not have noticed. She parked her rental car up the street, pulled off her shoes, and ran after him out the dock, and when she was right behind him put the gun to the base of his skull and pulled the trigger. The noise shook her up—not a man falling dead at her feet, no, but the noise—and then she heard someone coming, and ran. She threw the gun away. She meant for it to go into the water, but now we know where it went. And she ducked into the shower rooms there, and shut herself into a toilet booth, and then when nothing happened, she peeked out, and the only human in sight was old Le lying dead, and she took a chance and ran back to her car."

He looked at Tracy. "Yes, counselor. She was read her rights. She waived the right to have an attorney present and gave the statement voluntarily." He smiled thinly. "No way could anyone have stopped her." He nudged a cassette recorder on the desk. "Listen to it, if you wish. You will see. All facts freely given, and much remorse, much weeping."

"She was full of remorse at Le's funeral," Dave said. "But I expect it's remorse for herself. It usually is." He got to his feet. "I have work to do."

Flores squinted. "What else is there?"

"There's Cotton Simes," Dave said.

"My people are working on that," Flores said.

"Call them off." Dave went to the door. "By now Don Pham knows what happened to Warren Priest. And if that doesn't bring him to me, the news about Thao will. And if Cotton's still alive, I have a hunch he'll bring him too."

"I want to be there," Flores said.

Dave pulled the door open. "Sorry, but my house is way out of your jurisdiction." He walked out.

Cecil was playing backgammon with Amanda and others at Madge Dunstan's house at the beach, which meant he'd stay the night, and Dave sat in the dark, alone. It was the last time. Once this night was over, he was through with the investigation game. Sig-Sauer dark and heavy beside him on the long couch of the rear building under the rafters, the high roof, he sat on the couch, smoking cigarettes, sipping whisky, and not looking at the face of his watch when his lighter flamed, not wanting to know how long he'd waited since that would change nothing.

Outside, the canyon had grown quiet. No more crickets shrilling love songs in the brittle, brown September brush. The muted roar of traffic that drifted up from Laurel Canyon Boulevard had thinned out. Now and then a car labored up Horseshoe Canyon Trail. At such moments, he sat up straight and listened. But all the cars passed. Or so he thought. Did he drop to sleep? Maybe.

Something woke him. Quick light footsteps on the pine stairs from the sleeping loft. Up on the loft itself, his ears told him someone dropped in through the open skylight and landed with a thud on the bed. Someone slid out a drawer of the pine chest where he commonly kept the Sig-Sauer. He snatched the gun up, jumped to his feet, jacked a cartridge into the chamber, drew breath to shout at the intruder. And from only a few feet away, the strong beam of a flashlight dazzled him, and a voice right behind him said, "Drop it, Mr. Brandstetter, please." Dave dropped it.

The flashlight came toward him. A lamp lit up at the end of the couch. One of the doll-boys stood there in a tight black turtleneck and jeans, pointing an Uzi at him. Another reached around him and scooped up the automatic from the couch. Another unlocked the door to the courtyard, and squat, pock-marked Don Pham came in, looking grim. He had Cotton Simes by the arm. Cotton had bought clothes in New York with Dave's money. Safari jacket, slouch hat. A doll-boy followed him, gun stuck into Cotton's back. The one who had been noisy coming in through the skylight now came down the pine plank stairs from the sleeping loft. He said something in Vietnamese—probably that he hadn't found the gun. Don Pham snarled at him, and he shut up. He sat on the stairs, Uzi across his knees, and watched.

"It was these two," Cotton told Dave. He nodded at the doll-boy by the lamp, the doll-boy at his back. "They were the ones that killed the men at the Hoang Pho."

Don Pham stared at him and grew red in the face.

"You have now killed not only your foolish self," he said in his grating voice, "but your friend here. Do you realize that?"

"He's not that easy to kill." Cotton's eyes were wide and frightened, but he gave Dave a grin. "You don't get old like him without you got the brains to protect yourself at all times. A nothing little pimp like you—you think he's gonna let himself die in your kind of company?"

Pham struck him across the face. The blow turned Cotton's head to the side. He stood that way, eyes closed, as if in a pose for his mime act. Don Pham said, "Sit down and keep your mouth shut. I am sick of your empty-headed chatter." He shoved Cotton at the couch. Cotton fell onto it awkwardly. "You sit down too, please, Mr. Brandstetter."

Dave sat down. Cotton was staring at him as if his heart would break. Dave told him, "Don't feel bad. He never meant to let either of us live anyway."

"Why did you send for me? You said—"

"I didn't send for you. It was Lieutenant Flores's doing. He and Mr. Pham here have a working relationship."

Pham's eyes opened wide. "We do?"

"Don't you? I'll believe you before I believe him."

Pham nodded, sat down on the raised hearth. "No, we don't. But he is a fool. I always know what he is doing. I have people in his office."

"But not in mine," Dave said. "That's why you're here."

"I should have killed you along with Carpenter on the docks," Pham said. "It will take me months, years, to find another Warren Priest."

"I do hope so," Dave said. "But you'd lost him, anyway, you know. When I spotted him, eating lunch at

Hoang Pho, he was discussing a deal with Chien Cao Nhu."

Pham squinted. "Chien Cao Nhu? The boat dealer?"

"You know him?" Dave said.

Pham shook his head. "I have only seen his name, on the sign at his place of business."

"It's a front. It was a front in New York State not long ago, but some rival there made things hot for him. Then a grand jury got into the act. So he came to California."

Pham grated out what must have been a Vietnamese curse. "Where is he? Why wasn't he arrested along with Priest?"

"For the same reason you weren't. The police can't find him. I expect he's out at sea," Dave said. "And won't be back for a while. Carpenter was working with him too—did you know that?"

Pham made a face. "I knew he was double-crossing me. When I saw those bank statements you got, I knew that. But I didn't know it was Chien. I didn't know who it was."

Dave raised his eyebrows. "You saw those bank statements? Ah. Your source in the police department found them on Tracy Davis's desk, and used a copying machine, right?"

Pham gave him a tight little smile that didn't last. "He was taking in twice what I was paying him."

Dave said, "Maybe you should have paid him better for his loyalty, when he killed Le Doan Ba for you."

"Carpenter was careless, and young Ba saw what he never should have seen. It was up to Carpenter to remedy his mistake." Pham snorted. "It was no proof of loyalty. It was to save his own neck."

"And yours," Dave said.

"Who was this girl who killed Mr. Le?" Pham said.

"It's a long story." Dave rose. "I'll need a drink."

"Please." Pham motioned him down. He called to the doll-boy on the stairs, gave him instructions in Vietnamese, pointed to the bar in the shadows under the loft. The small figure went where he was told. Bottles and glasses and ice clinked back there. Pham said, "Nguyen is her family name. But it is as common as Smith in this country. It told me nothing. She had been here some weeks before Rafe happened to mention her to me. And all he knew was that she was a cause of family friction. Why did she kill Mr. Le?"

"Her father was a cabinet member in Saigon in the last days before the U.S. withdrew from Vietnam. He escaped with a lot of money the U.S. claims he had no right to."

Pham tilted his head. "Escaped?"

"To Paris. He can't come to the U.S. or they'll prosecute him for embezzlement. But he evidently wanted to do business here, and since his sons were killed in the war, he sent his daughter. Thao."

"Why to the Les?" Pham said.

Dave began explaining. The boy in black brought a tray with drinks. Pham's was tall—vodka, gin? The others were whisky on ice in short glasses. One for Cotton, one for Dave. Dave drank from it. It wasn't his best whisky. He lit a cigarette, went on with the story, down to the point of Le Van Minh's murder. Then he said:

"But you wanted to protect Mr. Le that night. You failed, but your young friends here followed him down to the Old Fleet with that idea—right?"

"I had been keeping a watch on him for a long time. He was friendly with Mr. Tang and the other who were plotting to fund shipments of heroin here from the East. This is my territory. I could not allow this."

"Mr. Le would have been killed at the Hoang Pho too, if he'd been there. Why wasn't he?"

"I told you before. He was a man of rectitude. When he heard what was being proposed, he wanted nothing to do with it. He was shocked that these pillars of the local Vietnamese community would consider such a thing."

"So why did you continue to watch him?"

"Nothing puts a man so much in danger as his unwillingness to tolerate the frailties of his friends."

Cotton asked, "Is that what Confucius say?" He had poured his whole drink down his throat in one gulp. It was bringing back his lost impudence.

Pham glared at him. Cotton popped his eyes.

Dave snubbed out his cigarette. "Phat and Tang and the other two in the plan were dead. Why go on guarding Mr. Le?"

"Who knew if the plan was dead? Perhaps others still lived who could go on with it."

"And they might try to kill Mr. Le to keep him from telling what he knew?"

Pham nodded. "And Mr. Le could be of use to me, if the plan was put in action."

"Of use how?"

"With a little prompting from me, he could expose the plan to the authorities and put an end to it. So . . . I watched over him. My agent heard Mr. Le shout where he was going when he left his house. But my agent's car wouldn't start. He went on foot to find a pay telephone to alert me. I sent two others"—he glanced at the boys in black—"to see that Mr. Le came to no harm. But the warning call had been too slow. He was dead when they got there."

"And they didn't even see the girl," Dave said.

"They left at once. They did not want to be accused."

He smiled wryly. "How ironic that Mr. Le's death had nothing to do with my interests. I had no need of you."

"Don't be too sure," Dave said. "You don't know yet who it was those wealthy men your troops here slaughtered at the Hoang Pho planned to finance."

Pham narrowed his eyes. He hitched forward on the bricks of the raised hearth. "And you do?"

"And you also don't know who would be brokering the opium at the Asian end of the operation."

"You're boasting," Pham snorted. "It's impossible."

"Check it out," Dave said. "You're Vietnamese. Don't you have friends or acquaintances or associates in France? Get in touch with them, and have them keep watch on Nguyen Dinh Thuc in Paris."

Pham was all attention. "The girl's father?"

Dave nodded. "If they watch his house, I think they'll see that he's got an American visitor. A harmless-looking, skinny old man from California."

"Nguyen sent the girl to become a U.S. citizen to front an importing business for him?"

"She'd look pretty selling bric-a-brac," Dave said. "While the skinny old man handled what was tucked away inside the figurines."

"Who is this skinny old man?" Pham said.

"Holland Carpenter." Dave snubbed out his cigarette. "Rafe Carpenter's father." Dave finished off his whisky. "He took a flight out from LAX to Paris the day after Le Van Minh's funeral. That was an interesting day. Did I ever tell you about it? I went down to the docks that day, to the Le warehouse, and I was surprised at what I saw. Rafe Carpenter, handing over a pair of attaché cases to Chien Cao Nhu, who had arrived in one of his glossy boats. The old man was there, helping Rafe out, dressed as a security guard."

"Damn Rafe Carpenter," Pham snarled. He made a

OPERADORA CIC, S.A. de C.V.

Reg. Fed. de Caus. OCI - 850524

CANCÚN, MEXICO

RESTAURANT BAR PALAPA

Folio N.º 76497

C 111-5 CIC

Fecha	Importe
06-01-91	

Sub Total	8300
Tax	1505
Total	10005
S.A.	
Tip	2000
Total	12 005

Firma/Signature

few comments in Vietnamese, and stood up. "Time to go." He glanced around the room. "We don't want to spatter blood all over here. The next tenants should not be faced with such a cleanup job." He caught Dave by surprise, yanked him to his feet. He was strong. Cotton jumped off the couch, bowled over the doll-boy assigned to him, and ran for the door. "Be cool," Dave called after him. He was worried the Uzis would start chattering. They didn't. Instead, another doll-boy stepped through the open door and pushed the thin black nose of his gun into Cotton's midriff, who stopped with a yelp. "No need to kill me," he said. "I won't say anything. Did I say anything before? I didn't tell the police. Not one word. I am a mime. My art is silence."

"You told Mr. Brandstetter," Pham said. He and his helper were hustling Dave along toward the door. The boys hiked Cotton out into the dark. Dave was next. He was in shirtsleeves, and the night air was chilly, but he didn't think it was any use to ask for his jacket. Pham slammed the heavy door behind them and pushed Dave ahead of him. "It's a shame after you have been of such help to me to have to kill you." Dave wasn't moving. Pham grabbed his arm and dragged him. He grunted the words out. "You would add luster to my enterprises. But I couldn't trust you."

Now they were passing the shingled end of the dark front building. They were in the narrow front area where the Jaguar stood, overhung by ragged tree branches. Then they were up on the crackled, potholed tarmac of shadowy Horseshoe Canyon Trail. And helmeted L.A. police with rifles stepped at them from every side. One of the doll-boys yelped and fired his Uzi wildly. For about half a second. Then he was on the pavement and lying still. The other doll-boys dropped their guns, and fell to their knees. Don Pham let go of Dave and raised his hands high.

"Don't shoot," he bleated. "I surrender."

Daylight was gray at the windows. Dave got up and switched off the lights in the cookshack. He opened the door to change the tobacco-smoky air. In some treetop, a mockingbird sang. Dave brought the coffeepot from the big stove and filled the mugs again. At the deal table, Ken Barker yawned, a wide and noisy yawn. He stretched. "Other men get cautious with age. You get more and more reckless. What if Tracy Davis had said the hell with you?"

Dave shrugged, tilted more brandy into his coffee mug, lit another cigarette. He was woozy from lack of sleep and the brandy made him woozier. "Then she wouldn't have rung up your department, and the cavalry wouldn't have ridden to my rescue, and I could stop wondering what I'm going to do with myself for the rest of my life."

Both men were beard-stubbly and bleary-eyed. Barker had plainly got a kick out of leading the swat team up here in the dark dead of night. He'd long grown weary of sitting at a desk while younger men saw all the action. When these same younger men had bundled Don Pham and his imps of hell off to Parker Center downtown to be booked, photographed, printed, and at least temporarily locked up, when Dave's and Cotton's depositions had been taken, and Cotton had hitched a ride in a patrol car to the loving arms of Lindy Willard on the *Starlady* at the Old Fleet marina, when Horseshoe Canyon Trail was its quiet self again, asleep and at peace—Barker had been keyed up and wanted to talk. And the two old men had sat here drinking coffee and yarning for hours. Maybe they hadn't covered every case they'd locked horns on in the long past they'd often grudgingly shared, but they'd covered a good many.

"It'll take some getting used to, retirement will," Barker said. "Hell, they've even got counseling services for it now, therapy groups, support groups, like for drunks and people who can't stop eating."

"God forbid," Dave said.

"If you keep letting the Tracy Davises of this world talk you into just one more job, you'll never give it a chance." He slurped some of the hot coffee, and pushed back his chair. "I've got to go back to work."

"Lucky bastard," Dave said.

"If I don't keep an eye on everything, they could make a mess out of it." Barker heaved his bulk up off the stiff chair with a grunt. "It's a big case, it's all over the fucking place. San Pedro County, Orange County, L.A. County. France, Vietnam, Cambodia, Laos, Burma, who knows. A cast of thousands. The language barrier." He buttoned his shirt collar at his thick throat and pushed up the knot of his tie. "And these organized crime types like Don Pham are slippery." He took his suit jacket off the back of the chair and put it on. His massive shoulders strained the cloth. "And their lawyers know every technicality in the books. Flores says nobody's ever been able to convict Don Pham of so much as spitting on the sidewalk."

"Warren Priest will turn state's evidence. With that, I doubt Cotton and I will even be needed. But, listen, about Flores"—Dave got dizzily to his feet—"he'll try to grab all the credit. Keep it, if you can, will you?" He walked with Barker to the door. "He's not a crooked cop, but he's incompetent, and he's already too far up the promotion ladder for the safety of the rest of us. All right?" Dave worked the latch, and pushed the aluminum screen door for Barker to go out. "And thanks for saving my life."

Barker stood on the uneven, leaf-strewn bricks, looking up at the big, old spreading oak, the sky growing light beyond it, and breathing in the fresh morning air. He didn't turn to Dave to say it, but he said, "I wish I didn't think you were deliberately trying to throw it away."

"Am I?" Dave frowned to himself. "Jesus, maybe I am."

"Think about it." Barker started to lumber off. He stopped. "Friends coming." Dave stepped out of the cook shack door to see. Cecil came on, tall, gangly, looking solemn and reproachful. Amanda walked beside him, not as tall as his shoulder, neatly made, pretty and clever, Dave's father's widow, young enough to be Dave's daughter. She looked worried. They'd heard reports of last night's doings here on the radio news, didn't they? No television news this early. Seeing them, Dave thought he didn't want to throw his life away. Barker nodded to them, and trudged on toward the trail where his driver waited in a city car, probably asleep. "Goodbye," Barker called.

"Goodbye," Dave said.